Karen Wheeler was born in England but emigrated to Tasmania, Australia where she has spent most of her life. In between travelling to many and varied places worldwide, which has taken her to all seven continents, Karen has worked as a nurse, project manager, data developer, consultant, and primary producer. However, writing has always been her passion, and this passion has now resulted in the publication of *Live Donkey, Dead Lion* (a narrative non-fiction story). *Uncle* is the first of her novels to be published.

To my adorable grand friends, Fletcher and Hadley, who show me every single day just how beautiful and rewarding friendship with the young can be.

Karen Wheeler

UNCLE

AUSTIN MACAULEY PUBLISHERS
LONDON * CAMBRIDGE * NEW YORK * SHARJAH

Copyright © Karen Wheeler 2025

The right of Karen Wheeler to be identified as author of this work has been asserted by the author in accordance with sections 77 and 78 of the Copyright, Designs and Patents Act 1988.

All rights reserved. No part of this publication may be reproduced, stored in a retrieval system, or transmitted in any form or by any means, electronic, mechanical, photocopying, recording, or otherwise, without the prior permission of the publishers.

Any person who commits any unauthorised act in relation to this publication may be liable to criminal prosecution and civil claims for damages.

This is a work of fiction. Names, characters, businesses, places, events, locales, and incidents are either the products of the author's imagination or used in a fictitious manner. Any resemblance to actual persons, living or dead, or actual events is purely coincidental.

A CIP catalogue record for this title is available from the British Library.

ISBN 9781035897605 (Paperback)
ISBN 9781035897612 (ePub e-book)

www.austinmacauley.com

First Published 2025
Austin Macauley Publishers Ltd®
1 Canada Square
Canary Wharf
London
E14 5AA

My sincere thanks and gratitude go to my beautiful husband, John, for his unwavering support and his acceptance of my need to occasionally withdraw into a world of fiction.

Thanks also to my amazing friends, George and Sharon, not just for giving me my grand friends (surely, the most beautiful gift of all) but also for all the kindness and support you have shown me over the years.

I also owe a debt of gratitude to Lynne, Tony, Anita, Jarrod and Bec, the best in-laws in the world.

And, I would like to acknowledge the work of Justy Philips and Margaret Woodward, for dreaming of The People's Library of Tasmania and giving me the strength to remove my manuscript from where it languished unread in the bottom drawer.

Prologue
1987

Hettie calls. Her voice is warm and soft but tinged with anxiety; there is no hint of reproach. Even so, I feel guilty. It is one, maybe even two months since I last phoned and it is close to six months since I've been down to visit.

'I'm sorry to trouble you, Joe.'

I know this to be true. I can picture her agonising for days, delaying as long as possible before picking up the phone. She'd imagine that I am too busy, that she should be able to manage on her own. Hettie and Uncle have been their own entity, an isolated island in the sea of society, for so long now that it is hard for them to break through their self-imposed boundaries and reach out to another person; even me.

'It's not a problem, Hettie,' I say, trying to sound reassuring while attempting to swallow my guilt. 'Is Uncle okay?'

'Yes, yes. Well, no, not really. It's still up and down, good days and bad.' Taking a big breath as though to gain courage, Hettie launches into the reason for her call.

'I was wondering if you might be able to pop down soon. I think I need to make arrangements for…well, for placement in a nursing home…'

Her voice trails off and I can barely hear the last few words of her sentence. But I know what they are and no matter how softly they've been spoken, the unthinkable has been said.

'Of course, Hettie. I'll come down this weekend. Work owes me a few days off, so I can stay through Monday and Tuesday.'

'Oh no need to put yourself out, Joe, there's no hurry.'

I'm pretty sure there is a reason to hurry and that Hettie is only trying to delay the inevitable, but I let her continue anyway. 'You and Clara probably have plans for the weekend.'

'No, nothing planned,' I respond as casually as I can. 'Clara is off for a girls' weekend, so I would have been on my own anyway.'

This is a lie, we had a three-day getaway planned with friends, and the extra two days off from work had already been booked to fit in with this. Clara will not be happy, but I can't do anything about that. If Hettie is actually asking for help, then help is needed. With arrangements made, I hang up the phone and go to inform Clara of the change in plans. As expected, she is not at all pleased but she is, at least, understanding.

With a small suitcase packed, I leave London at eight on Saturday morning. The route is a familiar one; I've travelled it many times before. The worst of it is getting the city behind me. The business sector gradually transforms itself into an industrial sector and that gradually recedes into a residential area. Initially tightly packed, the houses eventually start to thin out, areas of greenery start to appear and I feel my shoulders start to loosen as my lungs drink in the fresh air.

Near Southampton, I turn off the highway, taking the smaller roads; relishing the feeling of space and freedom. By half eleven, I reach Charmouth in Dorset. Exiting off the A35, I turn into The Street, travel for half a mile further and then take another left into Stonebarrow Lane. The laneway, once dirt, is now sealed. Uncle's cottage is a mile from the turn off on the right. Pulling up in front of it, I step out of the car and stretch. I feel slightly done in from the drive, and my whole being seems to tingle with apprehension about what faces me inside. But there is also that wonderful sense of coming home; of returning to where I had always been so happy.

Reaching into the back seat for my suitcase, I lock the car and make my way to the wooden picket gate. The cottage looks essentially unchanged from my first visit, well over twenty years ago now; just a little rougher around the edges maybe. Jess, the black and white border collie, is asleep on the porch, ostensibly guarding the house, though she has yet to become aware of my presence. A home for two old people, and one old dog, that's what this cottage is about, what it has always been. At one stage, it had been a home for a lost and lonely child as well, but it will be none of that for much longer.

With a loud sigh, I acknowledge to myself that I might soon lose what is most important to me, but what I have shied away from for too many years. I lift the latch and the gate opens, the squeak of it swinging on its hinges is a sound that is finally audible to Jess. Rousing herself stiffly to her feet, she trots down the path towards me and once again I am greeted by a creature that is all tongue, teeth, and wagging tail.

ID# Part 1

Chapter 1

I was five the first time I went to stay with Uncle. He was old even then, or so he seemed to me. I caught the bus down from London by myself; a four-hour journey filled with trepidation. My mother walked me to the bus station, her trim body upright and determined, one hand grasping my suitcase and the other hand clasping mine. I knew, even at that tender age, that this was not for my reassurance, not even for my safety, but simply because she liked to be in control.

We arrived, as we always did when we went anywhere, at the bus station with plenty of time to spare. Having told me to wait by the door, Mother joined the ticket queue. I stood there, silent and pensive, fighting back tears, for what seemed like ages but could have been no more than four or five minutes. Appearing again at my side, my mother grasped my hand and walked me over to the doorway to the gents' toilet.

'Best go now because you won't get another chance until Charmouth,' she said dropping my hand.

I didn't move. Not because I thought I couldn't manage a wee, I had been just before we left home and I knew from past experience that I'd always be able to produce at least one drop of urine if Mother said I had to. I didn't move because I'd never been into the gent's toilet alone before. I'd either been accompanied in by Father or quickly ushered into the ladies' toilets with Mother. Sensing the reason for my hesitation, Mother waved me in dismissively.

'Go on with you. You've got to learn to do these things by yourself now. I won't be around to baby you this summer.'

I turned away obediently, my lower lip trembling. This was it then; not only was I being banished, but my period of exile was to last all summer. Even worse, it would commence immediately.

When I heard the news about going to stay with Uncle, I had not thought I would travel there alone. I'd assumed that Mother would at least see me safely there, but apparently not. I did wonder briefly if this was how Father had understood it would be, but couldn't decide whether he had or hadn't.

There were two other men already lined up at the urinal when I entered the toilet and a third man barged past me to take the spare spot between them. The door to the only cubicle was closed and I heard a grunt of exertion coming from within. Feeling intimidated in this environment, I decided I didn't really need to wee at all. Moving over to the hand basin, I let a bit of cold water trickle over my fingers and gave them a quick shake to dry.

'Did you wash your hands?' my mother asked when I re-joined her.

'Yes, Mother,' I answered dutifully slipping my still damp hand into hers.

Satisfied, she moved towards the bus parking bays at the back of the station where two buses stood silently waiting. Checking the signed destination in the window at the top of the bus, we walked past the first bus to stand near the second. Still grasping me in one hand and my suitcase in the other, Mother waited silently for the driver to appear.

After a few minutes, other passengers started to gather; all adults, milling around listlessly. I looked around me cautiously wondering who'd be on my bus and who'd be catching the other one. The other passengers were mostly women with only four men amongst them. Everyone was travelling alone, with no eye contact and no conversation to break the tenseness of the atmosphere. Even Mother, who usually liked to talk to anyone, kept her distance and tensed slightly if anyone came near her.

I was thinking, hopefully, that maybe some of the women would be travelling on my bus, for I generally found women responded more kindly to children than men did, when suddenly, a door at the back of the bus station opened noisily and a portly man in a suit, waistcoat, and cap appeared. He dodged his way through the small crowd and opened the door to the first bus with a long, thin metal key.

'All aboard for Dartmoor,' he called cheerfully as he alighted the steps and took his seat behind the steering wheel. The majority of those waiting, including the women, surged towards his bus. I watched the ladies pass by me, feeling ever-deepening dismay.

'Stop staring. It's rude to stare,' my mother hissed, yanking on my arm.

'Sorry,' I said looking up with what I hoped was contrition.

'Oh, for goodness' sake, what's that you've got on your face?'

Setting my suitcase at her feet, Mother rummaged in the pocket of her good coat with her free hand finally producing a white, unused handkerchief. With a deft gesture, she raised it to her lips and discreetly spat into the centre of the piece of linen. Dropping my hand yet again, she grasped my face under the chin with her strong fingers and proceeded to wipe roughly at a spot on my left cheek, not far from the corner of my mouth.

'You've got to learn to check yourself in the mirror before you go out,' she said still scrubbing vigorously. 'You can't appear in public with half of your breakfast still on your face. I'm not going to be there to do it for you, you know,' she added, as though the gravity of my impending exile had somehow managed to slip my mind.

Behind us, the bus roared into life and was reversing out of the parking bay. Within minutes, it was gone and my mother and I, along with four other gentlemen, were left waiting in silence again. With so few people on my bus, it seemed obvious to me that my destination was not going to be as appealing as Dartmoor. It was only years later that I learnt the irony behind that thought. The other bus was the visitors' bus for those with friends and family at Dartmoor Prison.

It is difficult for any child of five to stand still for long and I was no exception. But that day I'd stood there without moving, ramrod stiff, barely breathing, hoping fervently that good behaviour at that moment might earn me a late reprieve. It was not to be. A second driver, dressed the same as the first but with a slimmer, although sterner, build had soon appeared out of the same door from the back of the bus station. He also produced a long metal key, which he inserted into the keyhole in the door of the remaining bus.

'All aboard for Exeter,' he called gruffly.

Picking up my suitcase, my mother shepherded me towards the now-open bus door. The four other men went ahead of us and disappeared deep into the interior of the bus while Mother deposited me in the first seat to the right of the driver.

'Now, Joe, you're to be on your very best behaviour. Do exactly as you are told, eat what is put in front of you and don't go asking for any more. Speak only when spoken to and always mind your manners. I don't want any reports of bad behaviour, do you hear me?'

Depositing my case on the floor at my feet, Mother then reached into the pocket of her good coat and produced a small white paper bag, which she thrust into my hand.

'There are a couple of sweets to eat on the trip,' she said before turning away and descending the stairs. 'He'll be met at Charmouth,' was the final comment she made; thrown curtly over her shoulder in the direction of the startled bus driver.

Without a backward glance, she headed towards the bus station exit and disappeared from view. The bus driver looked from me, a little boy with one small tear slowly sliding down my cheek, to my mother's retreating figure and back to me again.

'There's no eating allowed on my bus,' he said curtly indicating a sign above his head. Then he lowered himself stiffly into his seat behind the steering wheel and with the turn of a key, the bus roared into life.

※ ※ ※ ※ ※

I only learnt that I would be going to stay with Uncle the day before I left. This was at exactly the same time I learnt that I had an uncle. "Mad Uncle Henry" my mother had called him, although that hadn't been meant for my ears.

The rule at my house was that I had to be outside playing, unless my mother expressly said that I could be inside. It was expected that I would appear promptly at tea time, with clean hands, just as Mother was putting tea on the table. I had a lot of trouble getting this exactly right; either appearing too early or too late. Sometimes this only resulted in an exasperated look from my mother, while at other times, it meant being sent straight to bed without any tea.

In an effort to always be right on time, I had taken to sneaking inside to the back porch, where a small hand basin, filled with cold water, a piece of soap, and a towel were always there for my father and I to use. Having washed my hands, as quietly and as thoroughly as possible, I would wait unobtrusively for the clanging sound of the saucepan lid being placed on the sink. This was my signal that it was the right time to make my way fully inside the house and take my assigned seat at the table.

This system had worked well for the past couple of weeks and consequently, there had been no more evenings spent lying in bed with an empty stomach. The unfortunate downside was that it left Mother free to concentrate on my other perceived shortcomings, such as tramping mud into the house or being too slow to get out of bed in the mornings.

On that evening, I felt that I'd been waiting an excessively long time so I opened the back door just a crack to see if I could work out what was going on. My father was sitting in his armchair in the corner of the kitchen, not far from the warmth of the stove. This was the usual place he'd sit during the evening, although he'd been sitting there a lot more frequently of late, even during the day. That past week he hadn't even gone to work, just sat in his chair by the stove while Mother, who was always busy, buzzed around him.

I was able to hear my mother's voice faintly in the distance and concluded that tea was delayed because she was talking on the telephone. This was confirmed by the loud rattle of the handset being replaced in the receiver and seconds later, my mother appeared at the kitchen door.

'That's settled then,' she said to my father. 'Mad Uncle Henry will have him.'

'Good,' responded my father, in that slightly breathless way of speaking he'd developed lately. 'He'll be right there. But you shouldn't call Henry mad, Helen.'

'Why not? He's as mad as a hatter.'

'Just mind what you say in front of Joe.'

At that moment, I heard the clang of the saucepan lid on the sink and so I slipped quietly in through the back door and into my seat, not really understanding what I'd heard.

'Have you washed your hands?' my mother demanded. She had her back to me but could obviously sense my presence.

I replied appropriately and our tea was swiftly put on the table. Mother had taken her usual seat opposite me while Father had stayed in his armchair; another thing he'd only recently taken to doing. He would rest his plate on his lap but didn't ever seem to eat much, just pushed the food around with his fork. We ate in silence, as usual.

Once we finished, Mother rose briskly to clear the plates away. She looked hard at Father's still half-full plate and then looked hard at him, but she didn't say anything. If it had been me, I'd have been told to finish my plate off quick smart; there was no wasting of food allowed in this household.

'Tomorrow you're going to Charmouth to stay with Uncle Henry for a while,' Mother said to me over her shoulder as she filled the sink with hot soapy water and commenced to wash the dishes.

'Who's Uncle Henry?' I asked timidly, fear creeping in around my heart as I realised it had been me they were talking about earlier. I desperately wanted to ask why I was going, but knew I'd only get a terse reprimand along the lines of speaking only when spoken to. I thought I might have a better chance of getting a response to a question about who this mysterious uncle was.

'He's your grandmother's brother; my uncle, which makes him your great-uncle I suppose,' Mother mused, relaxing slightly as her mind slipped back nostalgically to the time when she had family other than Father and me.

'I have a grandmother?'

This was news to me. As far as I knew, I had no family other than my parents. Mother pursed her lips and cast a stern look in my direction. This was what she did whenever I asked a question that she didn't want to answer. Obviously, my grandmother was a taboo subject.

'Am I to call him Uncle Henry or Great-Uncle Henry then?'

'You can call him Uncle.'

'But if he's my great-uncle…'

I usually knew better than to argue with my mother but on that day, I think it was fear that made me push the point. I was being sent away, I had no idea why, where, or even really to whom, and I knew I couldn't ask the questions to get the answers that I really wanted to know. So, I pushed this silly point just enough for Mother to lose her temper.

'For heaven's sake, Joe, I told you just to call him Uncle.'

Exasperated, my mother threw down the tea towel she was using to dry the dishes and headed towards the kitchen door.

'I'll get your suitcase packed,' she said as she left. Father and I waited quietly as her footsteps disappeared up the stairs.

'Come here, Lad,' he said to me gently when we could safely hear Mother banging cupboard doors in the room above us.

I slipped from my seat and made my way to my father's armchair. He quietly opened his arms to me and I scrambled comfortably into his lap, letting my head rest against his chest.

'There, there, Joe,' he said gently running his hand over my head, smoothing down my wayward hair. 'Uncle Henry lives by the seaside, you'll be going for a nice holiday is all.'

'But I don't know him.'

'No. But you soon will. I've met him once, it's a long time ago now before you were born, but he seemed like a very nice man. You're going to have a fun time with him.'

'Can't you come too?'

'Sorry Joe, your mother and I have a few things to do here. They won't be fun for you. That's why we thought you'd prefer to have a nice holiday away.'

'But Uncle gets angry.' My voice had dropped almost to a whisper at this point and my father put his head down closer to mine to hear what I was saying.

'Angry?'

'Yes, I heard Mother call him mad Uncle Henry like he's always mad at people.'

'Ah,' said my father and with my ear pressed against his chest, I could hear the wheeze of his breathing as he did so. 'She didn't mean mad as in angry. She meant mad as in…well, not conventional.'

'What does that mean?'

'It means he doesn't always act like a grown-up even though he is one. That's why I think you're going to have fun, it'll be like having an older brother to play with.'

I stayed sitting on Father's lap until Mother returned and ordered me to bed. His words had calmed some of my anxieties but they'd still not given me an explanation about what I'd done that was so terribly wrong. Try as I might, I could think of nothing that was so bad it meant I should be banished.

Chapter 2

The bus journey passed in a blur. I remember us making several stops and people getting on the bus, but I can't remember anyone getting off. No one sat next to me, so I remained on my own for the entire journey; a little boy dressed in grey school shorts, jumper, cap, and socks with black school shoes. I don't recall why I was wearing my school uniform, for it was still three months before I would commence going to school. Maybe they were the only smart clothes I had, purchased only two days earlier and never worn before.

I don't remember feeling hungry during the four-hour journey. I was still clutching the white paper bag, but I felt no temptation to eat the sweets inside, despite the fact that they were a very rare, and much desired, treat. It was not just the stern warning I'd received from the bus driver that put me off; I was simply too wrapped up in my own misery to have any appetite. I do, however, remember feeling a desperate longing to go to the toilet. Mother had been right, as always, I should have gone at the bus station in London.

The pain in my bladder had been strangely beneficial; it helped to take my mind off the total sense of abandonment that threatened to swamp me. It eventually consumed all of my thoughts and replaced my vague fear that I had been deserted with a very real fear that I might wet my pants.

The bus pulled over again, this time in a small street in what seemed like the middle of nowhere. I hadn't been consciously following our route for some time now and wasn't aware that we had turned off the highway. The door opened and a man stepped inside, just onto the first step. He peered over the metal barrier between my seat and the stairwell. A pair of crystal-clear blue eyes peered at me from under a shaggy mop of grey hair. His eyes darted to the empty seat beside me, the fact of which brought a look of surprise and then a frown to his face, before they turned back to me and a beaming smile replaced the frown.

'I guess you must be Joe.'

A good ten years after this, the BBC produced a children's drama series called *"Catweazele"*. I remember watching the show for the first time and thinking they must have modelled the title character on Uncle; for he looked just like him. The man before me was thin and wiry in build. He had a hairstyle that could best be described as a bowl cut gone wild. His small goatee beard and moustache were also grey, with the beard trimmed slightly lopsided. He wore a long coat of a greyish-white colour, which hung loosely at the front.

His question startled me from my serious consternation over my ability, or lack of ability as the case may be, to keep control of my bladder for very much longer. My first thought was that this was not the uncle I had expected to see. As I've grown older and gathered a better understanding of the term "unconventional", I can see how apt my father's description was. But back then, aged five, I'd focused more on the description of his being not gown-up and so I'd expected to see someone who looked like an older brother-type version of me. The man in front of me just looked old.

I did not respond to his question, merely looked dumbly at him.

'Come on, I haven't got all day, there's a schedule to keep to you know,' grumbled the bus driver, staring at me sternly.

'Are you Uncle?' I finally managed to stutter.

'Yes, that's me,' he responded with a cheery grin.

Reaching over the barrier, he grasped the handle of my suitcase and hoisted it back to hang by his side. 'Come on then, Lad,' he said holding out his other hand to me.

It was the use of the term "lad" that finally spurred me up and out of my seat. My father rarely called me Joe, mostly I was just "Lad". My longing for him, even for my mother, intensified greatly at that moment. But they were not here so there was nothing else for it but to move. With Uncle's help, I clambered down the stairs onto the verge of the road. Behind me, the bus door slammed shut and the bus roared away.

'What have you got there?' asked Uncle, indicating the white paper bag I still had clutched in my hand.

'Sweets,' I responded feeling a lump start to form in my throat and tears well in my eyes. 'The bus driver said I wasn't allowed to eat them on his bus.'

'Why, you must be starving then?'

I shook my head vehemently no, and as the tears finally started to fall in earnest, I managed to choke out that I really needed to go to the bathroom and that I didn't want to wet my pants.

Uncle crouched down in front of me, his deep blue eyes level with mine.

'Well, here's what we'll do, Joe. We'll put those sweets in your pocket for later.' Taking the packet from my hand, he did exactly that, tucking them in firmly. 'There's no point eating them now because we've got scones waiting for us at home and I bet by the time we reach home, you will really be starving. Now let's talk about the bathroom problem. Are you really busting?'

I nodded yes.

'Well, of course, you are, you've had four hours on that bus, it was silly of me to ask. Hmm, let's see.' Uncle looked around him briefly before turning back to me.

'I've got it. We'll step over to that bush over there and you can pee there. It'll be just like you're giving the plant a drink of water.'

'Mother wouldn't like me to do that,' I managed to hiccough out between sobs.

'No, you're right, she probably wouldn't, but then she's not here to know about and I'm not going to tell her if you don't.'

Still, I hesitated.

'Tell you what, how about I go first and that way we'll both have done something that Helen, your mother, wouldn't approve of. It'll be like we're partners in crime.'

Pleased with his suggestion, Uncle jumped up and strode over to the nearby bush. With a quick glance around to make sure no one was coming, he fronted up to the tree. Seconds later, a stream of urine hit the ground between the trunk of the tree and his shoes.

'Give a yell if you hear someone coming,' he called to me over his shoulder.

I was so taken aback by watching my uncle urinate into a shrub by the side of the road that I immediately stopped crying.

'Right your turn,' he said straightening his clothes and turning back to me. 'I'll keep a lookout for you.'

Tentatively, I stepped towards the bush and with my back to Uncle, opened the front of my shorts. At first, I thought I wouldn't be able to go, thoughts of my mother's disapproval might hold me back, but the pressure in my bladder was too great. The relief was immense. Once finished, I reclad myself and turned back to Uncle.

'Well done,' he beamed as though I had just achieved something spectacular. Which I knew I hadn't; I'd actually done something really bad. But so had Uncle and he was an adult so that made me feel that maybe it wasn't too bad a thing to have done.

Picking up my suitcase, Uncle commenced to walk along the road, following the direction the bus had taken.

'Come on then, let's get you home so we can tuck into those scones.'

With no other option open to me, I followed Uncle, scurrying slightly to catch up.

'Do you like scones? I do, they're my favourite. Although I do like custard tarts equally as much and, actually, when I think about it, I am rather partial to chocolate éclairs, too. What about you?'

We'd reached a junction in the road and Uncle turned left into a narrow dirt laneway. He strode along, taking long steps which I had no chance of matching. I felt I had to take three steps to his one. I was still slightly breathless from my fit of crying and within minutes, had started to pant with the effort of keeping up.

'I don't know,' I managed to say between gasps. 'I've never eaten any of those things, at least I don't think I have.'

'What!' shouted Uncle, stopping suddenly and turning to face me. He swung my case around as he did so, almost knocking me off my feet. Scared that I'd done something wrong, I retreated a few paces for safety's sake. Uncle seemed unperturbed by my reaction.

'That's dreadful,' he said and immediately resumed his rapid walk along the laneway. 'We'll have to remedy that. Today, we'll have scones and tomorrow it'll be custard tarts and then chocolate éclairs the day after that. It's a good thing you've come for the whole of summer, that will give me lots of time to introduce you to all the yummy things in life. It's not right that a young boy like you has missed out on these delights. Whatever is Helen thinking?'

I had trouble keeping up with his rapid train of thoughts, but I understood enough to know that if he was angry, and I wasn't sure that he really was, then he was angry at Mother not at me. Not understanding the concept of rhetorical questions though, I felt the need to answer him.

'I don't know, Uncle, but Mother does say that sweet things are bad for your teeth.'

'Yes, I've heard that said as well, but my teeth are fine and I eat cakes and puddings every day.'

To prove his point, he turned to look down at me, gave a big grin, and tapped at his front teeth with a finger on his free hand. 'See no holes or breaks.' Uncle then looked up into the sky, gave a startled gasp, and increased his pace even more. Lost in my reverie, imagining being able to eat cake every day, I was momentarily left behind.

'Half three already,' he called over his shoulder. 'Hettie will be wondering where we are and the scones will be getting cold.' My trotting pace rapidly increased to a canter as I tried vainly to catch him up.

'Who's Hettie?'

Uncle stopped suddenly again, observing me as though I was the most remarkable thing he had ever seen.

'Hettie is my wife of course. Didn't Helen tell you about her?'

'No,' I responded honestly, not sure if it was me or my mother who was in trouble now. Remembering Mother's words that it was always best to be honest, I also confessed that I hadn't known about him either until Mother told me yesterday afternoon.

'Really? How odd.' Uncle resumed his walk, but his pace was not as fast as before. 'How very odd indeed.'

We continued at a more leisurely pace for another five minutes or so, this time without any conversation, until we reached a long stone wall with a wooden picket gate about halfway along. Uncle stopped at the gate, reached over, and released the latch.

'Here we are,' he sang out cheerily as the gate swung creakily open and with a small wave he indicated that I should go first.

The first sight to greet me as I stepped through the gate was a large, furry, brown and white dog charging straight towards me. I was sure its teeth were just about to clamp around my head when I managed to scamper back out the gate to hide behind Uncle's legs.

'This is Floss,' said Uncle, totally unfazed by me cowering behind him. 'She won't hurt you,' he added finally registering that I was not feeling very comfortable around the animal. I was not convinced by his reassurances and stayed firmly hidden behind him.

'Sit, Floss,' commanded Uncle.

Floss sat, her long pink tongue licking the teeth and lips of her lower jaw. Uncle turned slightly, exposing me to the dog's keen stare. The creature did not lunge at me.

'She just wants to say hello. If you just give her a pat, she'll be your friend for life. Here, let me show you how.'

Uncle reached out his hand and placed it under Floss's nose, letting her smell him. With a big slurp, the dog's pink tongue wrapped itself around Uncle's hand. Next, Uncle moved his hand slowly and gently to the top of the dog's head to give her a rough caress. Floss made no attempt to bite him, just looked at him adoringly with big brown eyes.

'Now your turn.'

Gently, Uncle assisted me in holding my hand out for Floss to sniff. When she got too close and I worried that she might bite, I tried to pull my hand away, but Uncle was holding it firmly, but gently, in place. When I did finally place my hand on the top of her head, to give her a gentle scratch behind the ears, I found her fur coat to be warm and silky under my touch. She looked happily up at me and I felt that I was safe for the moment at least.

'Good girl,' cooed Uncle patting Floss again. 'Well, that was easy enough, but now, you'd better come and meet the real monster of the house. We'd better not keep Hettie waiting any longer, she'll be wondering where we got to.'

With that, he strode along the path towards the front door and I followed anxiously with Floss trotting at my heels.

※※※※※

Hettie was waiting for us in the hallway. She was slightly shorter than Uncle and definitely rounder; not that she was fat, just soft and warm in her bodily proportions, exactly like her nature. She smelt of freshly baked goods, still warm from the oven and I instantly loved her.

'Hello, Joe,' she said.

Her hands and arms twitched by her side, as though she wanted to reach out and hug me, but sensing that this might be too much for me this soon in our meeting, she resisted.

'Welcome to our home.'

'Thank you,' I replied, remembering my manners.

Behind us, Uncle closed the front door. Hettie looked up and moved as though to greet someone else but stopped short when she saw there was no one else in the hallway besides Uncle and me.

'Where's Hel…' she began, a startled look on her face.

'Now Hettie,' interrupted Uncle, cutting her off before she could finish her sentence. 'Don't go being all nice to the lad and ruining my story. I've just been telling Joe that he needn't be afraid of Floss, you're the real monster in this house.'

'Oh Henry, you're incorrigible,' she responded, the cheery smile quickly returning to her face.

Lifting up her arms in an attempt to pat her bird's nest hair bun back into place, she looked back to me and asked if I'd like to see my room.

'Plenty of time for that later,' instructed Uncle. 'The lad's starving because the mean bus driver wouldn't let him eat his sweets on the bus.'

To confirm what Uncle was saying, I pointed to my pocket where the edge of the white paper bag was just visible.

'Uncle said to put them there and save them for later,' I solemnly informed Hettie.

'Good idea,' she readily agreed. 'Come on then, the scones are just out of the oven.'

We entered the front room of the cottage, a comfortable and cosy room where I would end up spending many evenings playing cards with Uncle and Hettie, or listening to Hettie read us a story. Under the large window, which looked out onto the front garden, there was a round dining table set for four people. Hettie ushered me into one of the seats and Uncle sat down opposite me.

After quickly clearing away the fourth setting, Hettie eased herself into a seat between the two of us. I was given a small mug of milky tea to drink and a scone, which Hettie deftly halved, topping each half with a dollop of jam and a healthy helping of clotted cream. It was delicious, absolutely so. From that day to this, I have never managed to find a scone that tasted as good as that one. Even other scones baked by Hettie have never quite managed to replicate that divine first taste of buttery freshness mixed with creamy fruit sweetness.

'Good, aren't they?' asked Uncle with a wink of his eye and I happily acknowledged that they were very good indeed. I must have been hungry because I finished my scone off very quickly.

'Would you like another one?' asked Hettie already reaching into the basket in which they lay snuggled in a red and white gingham cloth.

I was sorely tempted, but remembering Mother's instructions as I had boarded the bus, I politely declined.

'I'm going to have another one,' said Uncle taking the one that Hettie had procured for me.

'So am I,' added Hettie, taking another one for herself. 'Are you sure you don't want one, there's plenty there.'

'Mother said I wasn't to ask for more,' I explained, surprised that they didn't seem to know the rules that Mother said all good people in society lived by.

'Ahh, but you're not asking, we're offering so that makes it alright,' explained Uncle.

I thought this over and concluded that what he said seemed right. Hettie obviously thought so too because without further ado, she had another halved scone on my plate and was topping both bits as before with lashings of jam and cream. Uncle's words had satisfied me that I wasn't doing anything wrong and I must confess that because of that, I took advantage of every offer of food that came my way over the following three months with Hettie and Uncle.

After we'd eaten, Hettie showed me around the cottage. The kitchen, at the back of the building, was warm and cosy with a large black range oven and a rustic wooden table. It was in this room that we'd eat all our meals from then on. The table in the front room was reserved for special events only. Upstairs there were two bedrooms and a bathroom.

'This is your room,' said Hettie, throwing open the door to a room at the back of the cottage under the slope of the ceiling.

It was neatly, but sparsely, furnished with a single bed against one wall and a wardrobe against the other. There was a chair under the window, which looked down into the back garden and out towards the sea. I never once sat in that chair, just used it as a place to put my clothes at the end of a busy day.

'Henry and I sleep over in that room there,' said Hettie pointing to a door on the other side of the corridor. 'So, we won't be far away if you need anything in the night.'

She then helped me to unpack the few items from my suitcase. My two spare shirts were hung in the wardrobe, the next-to-best pair of shorts and another jumper were placed on the shelf below where the shirts had been hung, while the single drawer below that was reserved for my spare handkerchief, two pairs of socks and two underpants. My pyjamas were folded and placed on the bed.

Within minutes, the unpacking was done and Hettie was storing my suitcase on top of the wardrobe. Taking my toothbrush and comb in her hand, we made our way into the bathroom where Hettie drew me a nice deep bath with warm, rather than tepid, water. Never before had I luxuriated in so much water, Mother never filled the bathtub more than an inch or two.

Having scrubbed away what little dirt I had accumulated during the day, Hettie left me to soak while she went back to my room to fetch my pyjamas. She was gone a while and during that time, there was a whispered conversation between her and Uncle out on the landing.

I didn't hear everything clearly, but I know the gist of what was expressed was concern that a five-year-old boy had been sent on a four-hour bus journey to stay with total strangers all by himself. It now became obvious to me that the fourth-place setting at the table had been for my mother, and that they had expected her to accompany me. Hettie, ever pragmatic, concluded the conversation by observing that nothing could be done to change what had occurred and luckily, nothing untoward had happened to me.

Rosy clean in my bathtub, I felt the shame of not having a mother who cared enough about me, and the tears threatened to overflow again. Forcing them down, I practised putting on my stiff upper lip. This worked for the rest of the evening, as we ate our evening meal and then Hettie and Uncle taught me to play snap with an old, worn, pack of cards.

But tucked into my bed, with the lights turned out, my stiff upper lip resolve left me and I tried to bury the sound of my sobs in the pillow. I still had no idea why I'd been banished from home and what I could possibly have done that was so bad to merit being sent away on a bus all on my own.

It wasn't long before Hettie was back in my room. She had changed into her nightie and dressing gown, and had let her long hair down from the bird's nest bun. Scooping me up in her arms, she sat down on the edge of the bed and cradled me half against the soft towelling collar of her robe and half against the bare skin of her neck. Her skin was warm and damp, she was obviously fresh from her bath, but she still smelt sweetly of freshly baked treats.

I cried for a while, stopping eventually more from exhaustion than from my sadness ebbing away. Finally, remembering my manners, I choked out an apology for being such a nuisance.

Hettie smiled down at me and rummaging through her pocket found a hankie to help me wipe away my tears.

'You're not a nuisance, Joe. It's hard to be away from home for the first time, it's okay to have a bit of a cry about that.'

'Do you know what I've done that was so bad?'

Hettie stopped wiping at my tears and lifting my downcast face looked me directly in the eye.

'You don't really think you're here because you've done something bad, do you?'

My abject look of sadness was enough to tell her that I did.

'Oh Joe, you haven't been bad. You're here with Henry and me because your dad's sick. You did know about your dad didn't you?' she added when she felt me stiffen in response to her comment. I shook my head, unable to speak.

'Well, you're not to worry about that. He's got a bit of a problem with his breathing and he has to go to the hospital to have an operation. Your mum is going to be too busy spending time at the hospital with him and then looking after him when he gets home. So, she and Gerald thought you'd have a miserable summer in London and it'd be more fun for you here with Henry and me. We certainly think it'll be more fun for us having you here to stay, rather than it just being us two crusty old folk here on our own.

'Now,' she said slipping me back between the sheets and tucking me in again. 'You're not to worry about a thing. You haven't been bad and your dad is in good hands with the doctors and nurses. Now wait here just a moment, I think I've got just the thing to make you feel better.'

Hettie left the room and returned after a few minutes with a soft toy in her hand. From the light seeping past the slightly ajar door to my room, it looked to have a black back and head, a white stomach and a small orange beak. It was a creature the likes of which I'd never seen before.

'This is Percy the penguin,' she said, tucking him into the bed beside me. 'Have you ever seen a penguin before?'

'No.'

'Well, he's a bird that can't fly, but he can swim really well. He comes from the South Pole and that means that he's a really long way from home, just like you. He knows just how you feel, so how about the two of you keep each other company while you're here?'

Percy was soft and fluffy and it felt good to have him lying beside me in the dark. Slipping my arms around him, I pulled him close to me so that we could both share the warmth of the blankets. Hettie stayed sitting on the edge of my bed, looking down upon me with a gentle smile on her lips, until sleep finally overcame me.

Chapter 3

'Joe. Joe. Lad, are you awake?'

Uncle's voice drifted over to me from the doorway where he stood in the dim light of dawn. I was in a state of half-wakefulness and had gained enough consciousness to realise that I was not in my own bed, but I was not yet alert enough to have remembered exactly where I was. Uncle's voice brought alertness and awareness crashing in.

'Yes,' I said sitting suddenly bolt upright, fearing I'd slept in or somehow done something else wrong.

Percy the penguin suddenly appeared in the midst of tangled blankets and sheets now piled around my waist.

'It looks like a fine day out. Would you like to go exploring?'

Like a red rag to a bull, Uncle's question evoked an instant response from me. Exploring! I had never been exploring before, and never really thought that I'd ever be allowed. Exploring was one of those magical things that Mother was sure to disapprove of.

Within minutes, I had scrambled out of bed, stripped off my pyjamas, and clad myself in yesterday's clothes, which Hettie had neatly folded and placed on the chair under the window. Dashing into the bathroom to quickly relieve myself, I was downstairs and into the back porch that jutted off from the kitchen before Uncle had finished putting on his shoes. He looked up at me and grinned.

'So, Joe, you have a choice to make. Shall we go and play at being Robinson Crusoe by exploring the beach, or shall we pretend to be conquering Saxons and clamour up Golden Cap?'

I needed no time to mull over which option I'd choose.

'Can we go to the beach, please? I'd like to see the sea.'

'Of course we can, Joe. Come on then, Lad, your wish is my command.'

Rising from his seat, Uncle reached to the hook near the door and brought down a floppy sunhat, which he plopped unceremoniously on his head. He then opened the back door and together, we stepped out into the beginnings of a new day.

We'd only taken a few steps when I heard the rush of feet scurrying towards us. Floss appeared out of the semi-gloom of the dawning light, her mouth open and her teeth clearly visible. Instinctively, I ducked behind Uncle's legs.

'Morning, Floss,' said Uncle, bending down to pat her on the head. 'You remember Joe don't you?' he added pointing in my direction.

The dog turned to look at me, its long pink tongue licking at its lower jaw. Floss stood her ground and I cowered in mine.

'Floss is never going to hurt you, Joe, she's as gentle as a lamb.'

'She could do; she's got big teeth.'

'It's not her teeth that you need to focus on. Look at her tail, what do you see?'

I peered cautiously past Floss's teeth towards her tail, which was swaying back and forth at a rapid pace.

'A wagging tail means she's happy to see you and right now all she wants is for you to say you are happy to see her too. Give her a pat like you did yesterday and she'll be content and leave you alone. But first, we'll let her know that you're the boss. Tell her to sit.'

'Sit,' I said feebly. Floss ignored me.

'You have to say it like you mean business, Joe. Let her know there can be no arguments, she has to do as you say.'

I thought of Mother, and how Father and I always did exactly as she said without question. Putting on my best mimic of Mother's commanding voice, I ordered Floss to sit. She sat, her tail still swishing frantically back and forth across the ground. Tentatively, I reached out to pat her like I had done yesterday. She did not bite me.

'Come on then,' said Uncle and Floss jumped to her feet and headed towards the bottom of the garden.

I experienced a brief moment of hesitation, for despite having spent the afternoon and early evening with Uncle, he was still a total stranger to me. But then he had helped me with the bathroom issue yesterday and, as promised, he hadn't told anyone about it, not even Hettie. He'd also helped me, twice now, in making friends with Floss, so I felt that I probably should be able to trust him. Uncle followed Jess and, not wishing to miss out on the opportunity of an adventure, I did too.

There was a small section of lawn in the backyard, over which two pieces of strong cord were strung, acting as the washing line. The rest of the space was taken up with garden beds. The ones closest to the house were Hettie's flowerbeds, while the ones towards the bottom of the garden were filled with an amazing array of fruits and vegetables. Along the back fence line was a row of fruit trees.

In the weeks to come, I would spend a lot of time here; planting, watering, weeding, and harvesting. But on this first day at Uncle's, I scampered through the backyard with barely a glance at my surroundings. Uncle opened the small picket gate in the back fence and all three of us entered into an enormous field of long grass.

'Is Floss coming with us?'

Despite my success in getting her to sit at my command and the fact that I had patted her twice without being bitten, I was still very wary of her presence.

'Oh yes, Floss loves the beach. Come on, it's this way.' With that, Uncle proceeded to make his way through the field towards a small rising hill in the distance. The grass only came up to Uncle's knees, but it was as high as my waist against me. Floss was often totally consumed by it, with only the white tip of her tail fluttering above it. I let Uncle lead the way, trudging along in the path of trampled grass that he made.

'Who was that man you said we could be at the beach?'

'Robinson Crusoe. Have you heard of him?'

'No. Is he an important man?'

Uncle laughed and reached down to tousle the uncombed hair on my head.

'No, Lad. He's a character from a story. He was a castaway, a survivor from a shipwreck washed up on a beach on a strange island. If this is your first time at the beach, I thought you could be like him, exploring new things, and making great discoveries.'

This idea pleased me. 'So, if I'm Robinson Crusoe, who will you be?'

'Hmm. I'll have to be Friday. He was a native islander that Robinson Crusoe befriended and he named him Friday because that was the day of the week when he first met him.'

'Did Robinson Crusoe have a dog?'

'No. No dog.'

'So, who will Floss be?'

'Oh right, Floss. I forgot about her. Now let me see, I think there must have been some sheep and cows and pigs there, so Floss can be one of those.'

I looked at Floss, pattering through the long grass ahead of Uncle. She was the wrong colour to be a sheep and too furry to be a pig. She was a bit small to be a cow, but that was probably going to be the best fit for her features.

'Floss can be a cow, but she'll have to be a baby one because she's too small to be a big one,' I announced, pleased with my solution.

'That would make her a calf because that's what you call a baby cow. I think that is a grand idea of yours. Right ho, Floss, you'd better start eating grass and saying moo,' said Uncle, but Floss just ignored him.

We continue to trudge up the long, slow incline. Uncle's stride was as long as it had been yesterday and I was soon puffing with the exertion of trying to keep up. By the time we were halfway up the rise, it was almost fully daylight. The sky above us was a pale blue colour, speckled with wispy clouds and streaks of red.

'There'll be a storm later today,' announced Uncle stopping to look at the sky above him.

I stopped to look too, but the day looked beautiful, with no storm clouds in sight. I reported this to Uncle.

'It's not the clouds that are telling me of the storm, but the sky,' he said, pointing upwards. 'Red in the night is a sailor's delight. Red in the morning is a sailor's warning.'

I nodded politely, but to me, the day still looked perfect, and nothing was going to ruin it.

We continued up towards the top of the rise. I could hear the sea before I could see it; a repetitive and regular pounding sound, similar to the sound Mother made when she was beating the dust out of the rugs from the hallway floor. In the distance, there was the squawking sound of birds, which Uncle would later tell me were seagulls. A salty tang scented the air around us.

Finally, I reached the uppermost point of the small hill and emerged from the long grass to be confronted by a neat walking track travelling perpendicular to the direction we'd come from. On the other side of the track was a small verge of grass, and then the ground just dropped away. I moved forward cautiously to peer down the face of a cliff, down to the beach below.

'Wow,' I said peering down the steep descent.

At the bottom of the cliff, I could make out the mixture of sand and rock which formed the narrow strip of beach. The tide was high and the wind was almost non-existent. The waves were low, rolling in lazily, rising to a small foot-high crest, and then slapping down onto the beach. I looked outwards and could see nothing but water, spreading before me for miles. The view was beautiful, but I was eager to go down and experience the beach first-hand.

'How do we get down?' I asked, half fearing and half hoping that we might have to scale down the rock face.

'We'll walk down the path towards the mouth of the river and cross over to the West Beach there.'

Uncle pointed away to our right and I saw that the path did indeed wend its way down the hill towards a fair-sized river. Floss was already some distance along the path, obviously, she was familiar with the route. Uncle and I quickly followed.

The mouth of the river, where it flowed over the sand and out to sea, was shallow, but quite wide. Over the course of this summer and many summers to come, the passage of seasonal time would be marked by the shrinking river flow, until finally, it would be little more than a trickle. To start with thought, it would always present something of a challenge for me to cross. I stood and looked at it in dismay and then looked to Uncle for advice.

Uncle was seated on the edge of the path, removing his shoes and socks and rolling his trouser legs up.

'Come on,' he called to me. 'This is the beach, it's always better to be barefoot on the beach.'

Putting all thoughts of Mother's disapproval firmly into the background, I quickly sat down beside Uncle, undoing my laces and ripping my shoes and socks off too.

'We'll hide them here,' said Uncle, tossing both our pairs of shoes carelessly into the long grass on the field side of the path.

With no further fuss, I followed Uncle out onto the beach.

The sand was damp and cool beneath my feet. Uncle led the way over the beach towards the breaking waves on the shoreline. Here, the passage of water from the river, over the sand and into the sea, shallowed a little making it easier to cross. I followed, unsuspectingly, behind Uncle as he waded effortlessly into the union between river and sea. The water was cold, so much so that I gave a violent shudder and stepped straight back out again.

'Watch out for the rip,' Uncle sang out over his shoulder, unaware that I was no longer following.

I presumed he meant for me to be careful or I might rip my clothes on something, but looking ahead, I could see nothing that I might catch them on. Uncle continued to stride through the water, his trousers rolled up to the safety of his knees, but the bottom of his coat dangling down and trailing in the water.

Gingerly, I tried the water again. It was still cold, but not as cold as before. I took a few tentative steps forward; the water rising slightly higher with each step. I could feel the coldness gently rising up my leg while my feet seemed to be getting slightly warmer. Mid-way through the river, the water rose to just over my knees; it had only been mid-calf on Uncle.

I could feel a tug, a gentle but persistent urge for the river to have me join it in its journey to the unknown depths of the sea. I continued to wade steadily and cautiously towards Uncle. I had almost reached the other side when I heard a large splash behind me. I froze sensing, rather than seeing, that there was a large creature looming out of the water with me in its path. Another splash and Floss darted past me, her tongue lolling, and her tail wagging, sending water splashing all over me. She bounded towards Uncle, seeking a pat of approval and just as I reached the other side, she threw herself into a full body shake, spraying both Uncle and I with salt water and sand.

'Floss, go over there and shake,' said Uncle, but there was no anger in his voice and Floss ignored him.

'That was fun,' I told Uncle when I finally made into onto dry land again. 'I've never walked through water like that before. It was cold and made my feet tingle and it felt like it wanted to carry me away with it.'

'That's the rip,' explained Uncle. 'It's gentle enough here but it can be very strong a bit further out to sea. Come and feel the waves breaking over your feet, that's even more fun.'

I followed Uncle down to the sea edge. I had to be careful; the beach was not pure sand, it was littered with small rocks and pebbles. The sand was pleasant to walk on, but the rocks were uncomfortable beneath my bare feet. Uncle seemed oblivious to them.

The rush of the waves over my feet was exhilarating. I couldn't help but laugh loudly and turn to run up the beach as the water rushed in and then turn again to follow it out as it ebbed away. This cycle repeated over and over again. In the years since, I've seen hundreds of children do just that, I understand why for it is pure instinct, a totally natural response.

I lost all thought of playing Robinson Crusoe and just revelled in the joy of running back and forth into the waves with Uncle laughing and urging me on. Finally, he persuaded me to stand still, to allow myself to experience the feeling of the spent wave receding and the sensation of it dragging the sand out from under my toes.

Floss followed me in and out of the water before finally wading in further than I was prepared to go and swimming round and round in circles. The developing waves lifted her up and then gently put her back down again. The strength of the water, to be able to pick up a dog as big as Floss, amazed me. Her presence no longer scared me, although I still maintained a wary vigilance on the action of her tail.

Finally sated with playing in the waves, I remembered that I was supposed to be Robinson Crusoe and began my exploration of the beach. With Uncle following my every step, we traversed the beach from one end to the other. Everything we found was amazing, simply because it was all new to me. Our finds included shells, seaweed, driftwood, dead fish, seagulls, crab holes, rocks, and litter.

Uncle wasn't happy about the litter, he said it was bad people who were too lazy to put rubbish in the rubbish bins that caused that. It was dangerous for the birds and sea animals because they might try to eat the litter and die. He filled his coat-pockets with the papers we found and later, at home, I saw him empty his pockets into the rubbish bin there.

I discovered that not all shells were the same; there were lots of different sorts to find. Uncle and I started a collection to see how many different sorts we could gather. By the end of the beach, we'd amassed twelve different types. There were a few different types of seaweed as well, but while they were interesting, I didn't find them beautiful enough to collect and keep.

We found a dead crab as well. Uncle said it was a velvet swimmer crab and it was called that because it was covered in short hairs, which gave it a velvety appearance. Uncle knew a lot about most things that we found and he shared that knowledge with me. He told me so much that I don't remember it all now.

At the other end of the beach, near the townships of Charmouth, we rested for a while, lying on our backs on the sand. I retrieved the little white paper bag of sweets from my pocket and shared them with Uncle. There were four sweets, two each. We guessed the flavour of the ones we were eating and discussed what our favourite flavour was. Uncle liked something called aniseed, while my favourite was strawberry. Uncle told me that he had strawberries growing in the garden and in a week or two, we'd be able to pick them and eat them straight away. That prospect made me glad I was staying for a while.

We then walked back along the beach looking for all the things we'd missed on our first exploration. There was heaps of stuff, including another five types of shells, and I wondered how we hadn't seen them before.

'The tides gone out,' Uncle explained. 'This was all under water before.'

I looked and realised he was right; the beach was much bigger and the waves were further away. The river crossing was shallower without the inward surge of the sea; the rip had calmed right down, too. We made our way across the wet sand out to where the waves now broke on the shore, and once again, we amused ourselves by running in and out of the sea. Uncle joined Floss and I this time, with Uncle and I both laughing, while Floss just barked loudly.

I was careful to make sure the bottom of my shorts didn't get wet because I didn't want Hettie to be mad at me like Mother would be. Uncle wasn't concerned though, the bottom of his coat getting splashed every time a wave rolled in.

Suddenly, Uncle stopped what he was doing, darted his blue eyes in the direction of the sun and announced that we should be off. I never saw Uncle wear a watch, never knew him to be fazed or anxious about doing anything by the clock, except for this one moment in every day. With a glance at the sun, irrespective of what was happening, he would cease what he was doing and return home.

'It's afternoon tea time. Hettie will have our custard tart ready by now.' Uncle rubbed his hands together gleefully and together we returned to the path along the edge of the cliff from where we'd reached the beach so many hours before.

It took a bit of searching to find our shoes, Uncle having done such a good job of hiding them in the long grass. In the end, we had to resort to asking Floss for help to sniff them out. She rustled through the grass, her tail wagging, and appeared triumphantly a moment later with my lost shoe in her mouth. We trudged back up the path and at some point, Uncle just knew to step off the well-trodden bare ground and into the field of long grass to make our way back home.

I was glad that the last bit was downhill for I was feeling very weary by then. Floss still bounded around with an inexhaustible supply of energy and Uncle's stride didn't slow down to match mine. It was a great relief to finally reach the stone wall back fence of Uncle and Hettie's cottage.

We had just stepped inside the gate and secured the latch when a loud clap of thunder reverberated across the sky from behind us. Floss yelped and raced away to the back door of the house.

'Floss is scared of thunder. You don't mind it though do you, Joe?'

I shook my head and turned to look at the sky. What had been a beautiful day was now dark and foreboding. Any trace of blue sky and sunshine was hidden behind heavy, dark clouds. A fork of lightning suddenly darted across the sky, reaching from heaven to earth, and the thunder sounded again. I could see a wall of rain approaching even before the first drop landed with a large plop on my shoulder.

'Red in the morning, a sailor's warning,' said Uncle repeating his words from this morning.

At that moment, I knew that Uncle was the smartest man I had ever met and that there was probably nothing that he didn't know.

'Come on, last one in is a rotten egg,' he said turning and racing towards the back door; his coat tails flapping behind him.

Another large drop of rain landed on my nose, followed by one on the top of my head and another on my shoulder. Laughing with delight, I turned and ran after Uncle into the house.

Chapter 4

We both tumbled through the door as the rain began to fall in earnest. Floss, not usually an inside dog, dashed past us to hide under the kitchen table as more thunder shook the air around us. Neither Uncle nor Hettie seemed to mind this. They seemed to understand that leniency was required in the face of such overwhelming fear, something I doubted Mother would sanction.

Hettie was standing at the sink, a black kettle in her hand filling the teapot. I was anxious for a moment, thinking we might not have timed our return just right, but Uncle continued inside without a second thought and Hettie gave me a welcoming smile rather than a look of exasperation. The table was set for three and I could see a tart on the table; golden pastry with a creamy yellow filling. The kitchen and Hettie smelt divine and my stomach rumbled audibly.

'Hands first please, boys,' she said as both Uncle and I launched ourselves through the door from the back porch. Fearing I'd miss out on some custard tart if I didn't mind my manners, I did as I was asked immediately even though Hettie's voice didn't sound nearly as stern as Mother's.

Hands washed, we took our seats, with me next to Uncle and Hettie opposite us both. Hettie cut the tart while Uncle and I watched hungrily. My slice was on my plate and Hettie had Uncle's suspended on the cake slice mid-way to his plate when she suddenly stopped what she was doing.

'Henry, did you give Joe any breakfast this morning? Did you take anything with you for his lunch?'

Uncle looked from Hettie to me and back to Hettie again.

'No. Should I have?'

'Yes, Henry, you should have. Poor Joe has had nothing to eat all day.'

I looked anxiously from one to the other. I didn't want Uncle to be in trouble, especially not on my account. I remembered from yesterday how Uncle had made himself a partner in my crime so that I wouldn't get into trouble for weeing in the bushes. I needed to find a way to get Uncle out of trouble now.

'It's alright, Hettie, I had my sweets,' I said, producing the now empty white paper bag from my pocket. 'I shared them with Uncle.'

'See, he has had something to eat,' Uncle announced triumphantly, obviously thinking he would now be off the hook.

'Oh Henry, you are incorrigible. Sweets are hardly nutritious and they're not enough to sustain all the energy you need for a busy day. Please don't take Joe out again without giving him breakfast first.'

'But he didn't say he wanted breakfast,' retorted Uncle, holding his plate out hopefully toward Hettie and the suspended slice of custard tart.

'Henry, Joe has the manners of an angel, which means he is never going to ask, he'll always wait to be offered. Do you promise to always make sure Joe has breakfast before you head out for the day?'

'Alright, I promise,' said Uncle jiggling his plate, a pained look on his face as he contemplated his afternoon tea being held just beyond his reach.

Hettie nodded approval and delivered the slice of custard tart onto Uncle's outstretched plate. Finally, we could tuck in and I had my first taste of custard tart. I thought it was delicious, just like Uncle had said it would be, and almost as good as scones with jam and cream.

When I went up to my room to get ready for my bath, I found my bed neatly made and Percy the penguin resting against the pillow. My pyjamas, which in my haste to go exploring with Uncle I had dropped untidily onto the floor, were neatly folded and tucked under my pillow. I felt guilty. Someone with the manners of an angel would not have left the room in the mess that I did. I resolved to be tidier and although my bed-making skills never quite matched Hettie's, I always left my room in the neatest state possible after that.

The evening passed much the same as the previous one except that after our evening meal, as the rain eased outside, we began to read a story that would last for the rest of my stay. Hettie had suggested cards again, but it was Uncle who got up from his seat and retrieved a book from the bookshelf.

'I think Joe might like to hear this story' he said, handing the book to Hettie. Finding her reading glasses from amongst the pile of papers on the coffee table, she looked at the title and smiled. Seating herself in the armchair, while Uncle and I made ourselves comfortable side-by-side on the couch she commenced to read.

'So, Joe, this story is by Daniel Defoe and is called *The Life and Strange Surprising Adventures of Robison Crusoe, of York, Mariner; who lived eight and twenty years all alone in an un-inhabited island on the coast of America near the mouth of the Great River of Oroonoque, having been cast on shore by shipwreck, wherein all men perished but himself, with an account how he was at last as strangely delivered by Pirates.*'

ଚ∙ଚ∙ଚ∙ଚ∙ଚ

I don't recall where we got to that night in reading *"Robinson Crusoe"*. Exhaustion overcame me and I must have fallen asleep on the couch and been carried up to bed. I do remember being enthralled with the story though. I was totally amazed at what that man was prepared to put himself through in order to live a life of exploration. Not only did he defy his father's wishes but he suffered terrible seasickness and was almost drowned on his maiden sea journey when the ship sunk following a dreadful storm. From my one day's worth of adventure, I now knew that there were many wonders in this world to behold, but I could only imagine what the world had to offer beyond our shores that would cause Robinson Crusoe to persist with his desire for adventure in spite of these early, and dire, trials and tribulations. I read the book again, only a year or two ago, and I can honestly say it still enthrals me now.

The next morning was just like the first; a whispered call from Uncle, me up and dressed within minutes, and no sign of Hettie that early in the morning. The only difference was that I made an effort to tidy my room. Folding my pyjamas under my pillow and retrieving Percy from where he had slipped under the bedclothes, resting him back against the pillow.

Uncle and I also had breakfast. Uncle was initially keen for us to finish off the custard tart from yesterday, but I knew that Mother wouldn't have approved of that and I doubted that Hettie would either. We finally agreed on a cheese sandwich instead.

I stacked the plates on the sink and followed Uncle out into another glorious day. There was no red sky warning this morning. Floss was there to meet me, her tail wagging frantically. I felt a little guilty to be greeted so enthusiastically, while in return, I was still slightly threatened by the size of her teeth. But I could admit to myself that her presence was no longer so scary to me.

All three of us played at being Saxons that day. We'd run up the hill from the top of the cliff towards the pinnacle of Golden Cap. Whoever reached it first had to yell out, "*I'm the king of the castle and you're the dirty rascal*", except for Floss who was allowed to just bark. Having conquered the world like this, we'd roll down the grassy slope and start all over again. After we'd done this three times, we had a short rest and stayed lying in the grass at the bottom of the hill, looking to see what insects we could find.

There were ants, which I knew from my home in London and grasshoppers, which I'd never seen before. We also discovered some bumble bees, and a cricket, which although I could hear it quite clearly, I could never actually find it.

Uncle had filled his pockets with dried apples from a jar that Hettie kept in the pantry and we sat on the top of the hill after our fourth ascent and munched on those. Now assured that Uncle was the foremost expert on everything, I began what would become an endless list of questions.

'Uncle.'

'Yes, Joe.'

'What are Saxons?'

'Uncle.'

'Yes, Joe.'

'What makes the tides come in and go out?'

'Uncle.'

'Yes, Joe.'

'What sort of beetle is that?'

And so it went on, all through this summer and the ones that were to follow. Uncle never seemed to mind. He never told me to stop pestering him, or that children should be seen and not heard. He always had an answer for me, even if it was to say he wasn't sure and we'd look it up the next rainy day. He never forgot that promise either. If we were forced to stay indoors at all, we would be found in the front room consulting the set of encyclopaedias or pouring over the atlas of the world. Uncle showed me in the atlas all the routes of Robinson Crusoe's journeys, and together we located the South Pole, where Percy came from; on the continent that was called Antarctica. Then we looked up some facts on both penguins and Antarctica in the encyclopaedia, all of which I relayed to Percy at night as I held him snuggled to my chest under the blankets.

When we'd finished playing at Saxons on my second day in Charmouth, we took a walk along the top of the cliff over a rocky outcrop. It was here that I slipped, my school shoes lacked good traction for this sort of terrain. I fell badly, skinning the palm of my right hand and scrapping both knees. The shock and the pain brought tears to my eyes. I received not one word of reproach from Uncle, either for being so clumsy or for sobbing like a baby. Instead, he assisted me to my feet, dusted me off, and inspected my wounds. He agreed that they must have hurt a bit and suggested we rest again until I felt better, which I did not long afterwards.

As a result of this accident, Hettie announced that evening that I was not to go out with Uncle the next morning, she was going to take me into the township and we were going to get some clothing and shoes for me that were more suited to the countryside. Consequently, the next morning it was Hettie who got my breakfast for me, showing me where the box of cornflakes was in the pantry and where there was jam and honey to put on my toast.

'Maybe you could help Henry do the breakfast tomorrow,' she suggested. 'He needs a bit of help with things at times. Just show him these things and save the cheese sandwich to take with you for your lunch.' I promised solemnly that I would.

The township of Charmouth was small in comparison to what I was used to in London. Here, all the shops were lined up on the main road, which was simply named The Street. There was only one small department store and it was in there that we bought two pairs of shorts, some shirts, and a light jacket. We also bought a pair of sandshoes and some bathers for me to wear when the weather warmed up. Hettie also threw in a sunhat, one just like the one Uncle wore.

It was decided that I might as well stay in the shorts and shirt that I had just tried on and so it was my school clothes and shoes that were packaged up while I slipped bare feet into the brand-new sandshoes. I worried about how I was to pay for all of this, Mother always said it cost a fortune to clothe me, but Hettie said not to worry, the change I'd bought about in Uncle was payment enough. I wasn't sure what that meant, but it sounded like a good thing, so I just let it go.

After we'd completed this bit of shopping, we made our way to the greengrocer, the butcher, and the baker. With all the purchases stored in the car, we then went into the cafe where Hettie treated me to a strawberry milkshake while she had a cup of tea.

This became our weekly ritual, the grocery shopping followed by our special drinks at the cafe. Uncle never joined us, Hettie said he didn't like coming into the town, didn't like a lot of people around him. After we'd finished our drinks, Hettie would let me look through the glass display cabinet to select a treat to take home for afternoon tea. With the morning spent in town, Hettie said she wouldn't have time to make anything herself. On this first trip, Hettie suggested that we take the chocolate éclairs, Henry had asked for some and she thought them much too fiddly to make herself.

We arrived home to find Uncle in the front room, pacing the floor. Hettie was laden with shopping bags and I carried a shoebox and a parcel of clothing from the department store.

'We're home,' Hettie called out as she passed through to the kitchen.

'Good,' responded Uncle, not coming forward to help her, a slightly pouty look on his face. 'Have you finished with him? Can I have Joe back now?'

'Henry, you are incorrigible,' said Hettie with a shake of her head but with a smile on her face. 'Yes, you can have Joe back now. Of you both go and play, I'll see you at afternoon tea time.'

Uncle raced towards the back door, and after rummaging through my parcel for my new sunhat, I quickly followed him.

Chapter 5

I think Uncle saved the best adventure until the last. Towards the end of my first week of staying in Stonebarrow Lane, Uncle, Floss, and I headed out early in the morning, as per our now usual routine. We made our way through the field of long grass until we again reached the top of the cliff. We strolled down towards the beach, but this time instead of crossing the river to play Robinson Crusoe on West Beach, we turned left and headed along East Beach to the base of the cliffs.

Here, we didn't really play at being anything, although we could have been either marine biologists or palaeontologists. We were simply Joe and Uncle poking in rock pools to see what inhabitants we could find, and lifting up rocks to see what lay beneath. We also searched the rocks for the fossils of creatures who'd lived long, long ago. I didn't know what a fossil was until Uncle showed me one that he found, which he said was an ammonite.

I thought it was a worm, wrapped in a tight coil and somehow hardened into rock, but Uncle turned it around and showed me how many people thought it resembled a ram's horn. He said it was the preserved remains of a sea creature, a relative of the squid, who'd lived possibly 65 million years ago. I struggled with that idea of time, for I couldn't picture how long 65 years would be, let alone 65 million of them. I just knew it was a very long time and even though this creature no longer existed, I was able to see an imprint of what it had looked like. That was truly amazing.

The days spent at this location were probably the happiest days of that summer, although not one single day of that period could ever have been called a bad day. On our wet days, spent pouring over the encyclopaedias, I'd be entranced by some of the pictures of the funny sorts of creatures that were alive today, creatures such as the platypus, the armadillo, and the elephant shrew. If I thought they were fantastic creatures, then I was totally in awe at the evidence we found of what had lived here millions of years ago.

In the rock pools, we found a variety of sea life such as crabs, prawns, starfish, and sea urchins. After a high tide, we'd sometimes find little fish, washed into the pools and who were unable to escape once the water level had fallen again. I tried to catch them in my hands, to carry them quickly over the rocks and toss them back into the sea, but they were too quick for me to catch. Uncle laughed at my antics and reassured me the fish would be okay.

'They'll swim out next high tide,' he told me and I hoped it was true.

The crabs were my favourite find in the rock pools. Uncle warned me about their pincer claws and how the crab could use them to give a nasty nip. Once I wasn't quick enough and ended up with a crab suspended from my finger. It did hurt, but I didn't cry that time. Some crabs had a serrated edge to their shell, while one of the crab shells looked like the piecrust edge that Hettie produced on the tarts that she made.

We also found some anemone, a seaweed-type creature with a big sucker it used to attach itself to the rocks. It had brown-green tentacles, with a blue bead on the end, and if you touched them, it would retract the tentacle away from your reach. I loved playing with them.

The fossils we found fell into a totally different realm of amazement from anything else I had discovered so far. Uncle explained the process of how they came into being, but knowing the science of the process didn't stop me from being totally in awe of the outcome. Some of the fossils we found were poorly formed and incomplete, while others were beautiful specimens, rich in detail. I loved to run my fingers over them, gently feeling the ridges and outlines of what had once been leaves, or shells or bones.

Uncle told me that a fossil of a dinosaur had been found along here and I stored a secret hope that there was another such fossil to be found and that I'd be the one to find it. We looked up the dinosaur in the encyclopaedia on one of our rainy days. It was called an Ichthyosaur, a dolphin-like creature with a long, flat nose much like a crocodile has today.

In this fashion, the summer passed. Uncle, Floss, and I rambled along the beaches, cliffs, and hills around Charmouth. When we weren't off exploring, we'd work in the garden, preparing garden beds, weeding, planting, and harvesting. Just as Uncle had promised, strawberries soon appeared, little plump red morsels of sweetness, which just seemed to melt in my mouth. The apricot and nectarine trees bore fruit. I ate too many one day and gave myself an awful stomach-ache.

Once a week, Hettie and I went down into the township to shop and then sit in the window seat of the café, Hettie with her cup of tea and me with my strawberry milkshake. When we returned home, we always found Uncle pacing the floor and demanding to have me back again.

Once a week, Hettie also called my parents on the phone. For the first few weeks, I only spoke with Mother. She never mentioned Father's illness, and because I only knew Father was ill through Hettie's slip of the tongue, I never felt I could ask about it. My conversations with Mother were always short.

'Are you behaving yourself?'

'Yes, Mother.'

'Don't forget to say please and thank you, and have you been washing behind your ears?'

'Yes, Mother. Uncle and I went fossil hunting today.'

'Well, I haven't got time to talk about that. Just make sure you don't do anything to disgrace me and I hope you haven't scuffed your new school shoes.'

I didn't tell Mother about Hettie's shopping spree for new clothes for me. This was not just because Mother would have been very angry, but also because my life in Charmouth with Uncle and Hettie didn't seem in any way connected to my life in London with Mother. It seemed appropriate to keep the two separate.

Uncle and I continued to explore the world through our experiences at Charmouth and what we found in the encyclopaedias and the atlas, and I kept up with my endless list of questions.

'Uncle.'

'Yes, Joe.'

'Why do some people grow taller than others?'

'How does water get into the clouds?'

'What does nutritious mean?'

When I look back at that time now, I realise that Uncle was the most patient person I have ever known. In fact, he was not just patient, he was also supportive and encouraging. He fed my thirst for knowledge, understanding that the more I knew, the more I would want to know. When I did eventually start school, I was not one of the brightest students when it came to writing and math skills, but I knew more about nature and the world around us than any of my fellow pupils and I could spell ichthyosaur, which they couldn't.

Uncle was also very patient and honest when it came to questions of a different kind.

'Uncle,' I ventured one afternoon after I'd been staying with him for several weeks.

'Yes, Joe.'

'Why have I never met my grandmother?'

This question had been on my mind ever since I'd discovered that I had a grandmother. From my limited experience, gained from observing two other boys who lived in my street in London, children who had grandmothers usually saw them regularly. Even Duncan's grandmother came to visit him once a year, and she lived in Scotland.

'That,' replied Uncle without the least hesitation, 'is because your grandmother is a very silly woman.'

'Oh,' was all I could think of to say in return.

'Alice, that's your grandmother's name, is my sister, but you'd never guess it, we're not the least bit alike. The reason you don't see her is because she got a bee in her bonnet over your mother marrying your father and she hasn't spoken to your mother since. Silly woman, not only has she lost her only child, but she's missed the opportunity of knowing you, her only grandchild.'

'Why did she get a bee in her bonnet?' I didn't really know what this meant, but I was more anxious to understand why rather than what.

'Because your father is an orphan. Do you know what that means?'

I shook my head.

'An orphan is someone without a mother or a father. I don't mean that Gerald never had parents, we all have parents because we have to come from someone. But Gerald's parents died when he was a wee little lad, maybe your age, maybe younger. They were killed in the war, during the bombing. Gerald was found wandering the streets alone. No one knew where he came from and no other family came forward to claim him, and so Gerald was raised in an orphanage, that's a special home for orphans.'

'What's wrong with being an orphan?' The only issue I could see was that it would be terribly sad and lonely.

'Nothing. That's why I say that Alice is a very silly woman. She has this thing about how one's family says everything about you. That's why she doesn't have anything to do with me. She's scared that people might think she's mad because she's got a mad brother in me. Helen did tell you I was mad didn't she?' he asked, with a merry twinkle in his eye.

I nodded.

'Good, don't worry I'm not really mad, they all just think I am and I'm happy for them to think that if it means they leave me alone. Anyway, Alice believes that there are only good families and bad families and that a good family should only marry into another good family. Because Gerald doesn't know his family, Alice can't tell if he's good or bad, and therefore Helen shouldn't have married him. But Helen did marry him and Alice hasn't spoken to her since.'

'Oh,' I repeated, not really understanding my grandmother's issues, but deciding it didn't really matter.

'Don't worry about it, Joe. She's a silly woman, anyone who'd throw away a daughter and a grandson is not worth worrying about. I've only met Gerald once and I can tell you just by looking at the man that he's a good one.'

I agreed with Uncle, my father was good. Happy to have had my question answered we went on with the pleasant pattern of our lives.

My sixth birthday came on the 17th of August. Hettie surprised me with a beautiful sponge cake, light as a feather and filled with whipped cream and strawberry jam. She'd decorated it with fresh strawberries and six candles. I was so thrilled with this, never having had a birthday cake before. There was also a present for me, lying wrapped and waiting for me by my place at the table when Uncle and I arrived home for afternoon tea. Uncle seemed more excited by the present than I was, but only because I was dumbfounded by the concept of being given a present at all.

'Go on, go on. Open it up!' he commanded.

'Henry, stop fussing, let Joe do it in his own time.'

Slowly, I opened my present and gave a little squeal of delight. It was an ant farm; a collection of sand caught between two sheets of clear plastic with a broad red plastic base to stand upon and a red plastic lid to stop the ants from escaping. Within this sand was a small colony of ants and through the clear plastic sides of the farm, I would be able to see the ants at work engineering tunnels and building their network of nests.

Uncle and I had spent many hours watching armies of ants busily moving from one place to another, popping in and out of the many holes that formed entrances to their nests and carrying leaves, food, and other things about. I'd expressed a desire to be an ant for a day, just to have the opportunity of being inside their colony and seeing what it was like from the inside. This present would enable me to do just that. It was perfect.

There was also a birthday card from my parents. 'Happy Birthday to a boy, who is six,' it read on the outside and inside my mother had written, 'Happy Birthday, Joe. I hope you are behaving yourself.' It was signed simply as Mother and Father.

I could see that Father hadn't signed his own name, Mother had done that for him. I'd been with Uncle and Hettie for nine weeks by then, but I'd only talked to Father during the last two weekly phone calls. I'd asked if he was well and he'd replied that he was. But his answer was always slow and wheezy, and his conversation was broken by him having to stop and catch his breath. Mother never let him speak for long, always taking the phone from him after a minute or two. Still, it always made me feel better to have heard his voice.

As the days started to shorten, the volume of water running over the beach and into the ocean from the river Char started to wane, the farmer cut the long grass in the paddock behind us to make hay, and the story of *"Robinson Crusoe"* reached its final end. His twenty-eight years in the lonely wilderness of his island off the coast of America ended, just as my return to the constraints of London was about to begin.

Chapter 6

'Your mother called today, Joe,' Hettie announced as Uncle and I tumbled through the door in time for afternoon tea. We were both in high spirits, with a chicken clutched proudly under each arm. I was a little distracted, fighting what seemed like a losing battle to keep my chickens firmly in my grasp, and so initially, I didn't hear what Hettie had said.

We'd found the four hens, three white and one brown, wandering around in Stonebarrow Lane. It had been relatively easy to herd and then catch three of them, but that was because Floss had been busy sniffing at something further down the road and the chickens had been calm and relaxed, unaware of her presence. Just as Uncle was sneaking up stealthily on the last remaining white hen, Floss appeared out of the grass, travelling at a steady trot, nose down, with a bearing straight for the chicken. Startled, she'd taken off down the road, clucking frantically and madly flapping her wings.

Floss, excited by the commotion, continued to pursue the fugitive chicken, while Uncle alternated between yelling at Floss to sit and stay, and in a calmer voice trying to call the chicken to him with a gentle "here chooky, chook, chook". I had been of no use, merely standing by watching and laughing at the antics. Eventually, Uncle managed to corner the chicken near a wire cage on the side of the road, something we deduced they must have fallen out of, and scooped the chicken awkwardly up into his remaining free arm. Still laughing over our antics, we had hastened home to show Hettie our bounty.

The news that my mother had called stopped us both in our tracks and wiped the laughter from our voices. Never once in the two and a half months of my stay in Charmouth had Mother ever made a phone call here. It had always been Hettie who picked up the phone and called her. I thought of my father and his raspy, wheezy voice and my heart skipped a beat with worry that he might be ill again.

'Whatever have you got there, and what are they doing in my kitchen?' continued Hettie noticing for the first time the hens we were clutching.

'Chickens,' I replied dumbly.

'They fell off the back of a truck,' added Uncle. 'We're going to keep them and collect their eggs.'

'What about the person who owns them?'

'He drove off and left them, so it's finders keepers I say. Besides, he can't have had them very secure on his truck for the cage to fall off, so he doesn't deserve them if he can't look after them properly,' responded Uncle.

'Oh Henry, you're incorrigible.'

Uncle ignored Hettie's pretend stern and glaring frown and returned to the subject that was most pressing on my mind, and apparently on his.

'Why did Helen ring?' I looked up at Uncle as he asked this question and thought he looked a bit paler than normal.

'Oh,' responded Hettie, looking a bit flustered and not meeting Uncle's eye. 'Apparently, school starts next week so it's time for Joe to be heading back to London.'

'But Joe can go to school here. He doesn't have to go to London for that.'

'Well, it's not just about school. It's been almost three months since Helen and Gerald saw Joe. The poor boy is probably missing his parents and I'm sure he'd like to see them and they'd like to see him.'

Hettie was partly right. I would have liked to see Mother and Father again. I especially wanted to see Father, to check on his breathing and to know if he was able to get out of his armchair by the kitchen stove and be the active man he had been just a few months before. But I wasn't sure that I wanted to go back and stay permanently, to actually live with them again.

'Anyway, he's not going until Friday so you've several days of fun left yet,' said Hettie brightly. 'Now, what are you going to do about those chickens?'

That night, in bed, I held Percy close and told him I'd have to be going away soon. I reminded him that coming to stay at Charmouth had been very scary because I hadn't known why I was being sent away, where I was going and who I'd be staying with for I'd never met Uncle. I hadn't even known that Hettie and Percy existed. But that had all turned out well. At least going home, I knew where I was going and why, and I knew the people I would be living with, so obviously that would turn out well too. I felt at the time that Percy hadn't believed me, for he was still lying in my arms when I woke up the next morning as though he was reluctant to let me go.

Uncle and I had three days left in which to run wild and play. With tacit agreement, we visited all our old haunts and repeated all of the games and activities we had indulged in during the first few days of my arrival. We also finished some work in the garden, harvesting the last of the tomatoes and turning over some new beds ready for winter planting. With much laughter, we also built two pens for the chooks. Our first effort was a dismal failure with one of the white chooks lifting up the poorly secured fencing wire mesh and walking under it to peck at the strawberries. The other three chickens had simply followed suit. So, we tried again and this time managed to contain them.

We didn't speak of my leaving, but the thought of it was always there, a chunk of sadness hanging like a pendant around both of our necks, banging on our chests near our hearts whenever we moved. On our last day together, we sat up on the top of the cliff and looked down on the people playing and fossicking on the beach below. I felt the time was right to ask the question that had been plaguing me since my arrival.

'Uncle.'

'Yes, Joe.'

'What does incorrigible mean?'

Uncle chuckled. 'It means I'm a bad boy with no chance of redemption. No matter how much Hettie scolds or looks crossly at me, she can't get me to be a good boy. I'm a lost cause.'

'Oh,' I responded. 'I don't think you're bad, or a lost cause. You've remembered to get my breakfast every morning! Besides, what you do isn't bad. Being bad is not minding your manners, or speaking when you're not spoken to, or coming inside before it's tea time.'

'Is that what Helen tells you is bad?'

'Yep. Whoops, I'm not supposed to say yep either.'

'Well, I agree that you should always be polite, but those other things don't make you a bad boy and you can do them as often as you like while you are here.'

It felt good for Uncle to tell me that, even though I knew that tomorrow I would be gone. For a moment, I felt a flood of despair run through me as I sat thinking of all the things that would no longer be; no Uncle to play with, no Floss to greet me each morning with a frantic wag of her tail, no warm smile and tasty treat from Hettie. But I was not allowed to indulge in these thoughts for long. With a glance at the position of the sun, Uncle roused me.

'Come on, afternoon tea time. I think it's scones and jam and cream again today.' Taking great long strides across the mown field, with his long coat tails flapping, Uncle was soon halfway home. As on the first day of my arrival, I had trouble keeping up with him.

That evening, as I luxuriated in the last full, hot bath I thought I'd ever have, Uncle and Hettie sat out on the landing and talked.

'I don't want him to go.' Uncle's voice carried to me easily. Hettie's voice was less distinct and I did not catch all of her responses, but I did manage to distinguish the phrases "selfish of us", and "needs to spend time with Gerald", amongst what she had to say.

For the first time since I arrived, I was unable to sleep that night. My bed was warm and cosy, Percy was tucked in securely beside me, and the light was on in the hallway, lending a comforting warm glow to trickle in around the edge of the bedroom door that was slightly ajar. On the chair, under the window, sat my suitcase ready packed for tomorrow. The clothes I was to wear, the ones I had worn coming here, were clean and pressed neatly, hanging over the base of the open case. In my mind's eye, I couldn't help but picture this as the mouth and tongue of a monster that was going to come and gobble me all up.

Eventually, tired of tossing and turning, I snuck out of bed, with Percy tucked under my arm, and tiptoed across the hallway to stand at the open door to Uncle and Hettie's room. Hettie lay closest to me, her face turned towards me, her eyes tightly closed and her lips slightly pursed, alternately tightening and relaxing as she breathed gently in and out.

Behind her, I could make out the figure of Uncle. He lay flat on his back, his eyes wide open staring vacantly at the ceiling. It pleased and distressed me to know that Uncle was also still awake. I was pleased to know that Uncle felt the pain of our parting as keenly as I did, but upset to know that I was the cause of that pain. Without a word, I reluctantly returned to my bed.

For my return journey, I was not to be travelling alone on the bus; Hettie would drive me. It was never said to me directly, but I knew both of them thought it was a bad thing to send a child of my age on such a long bus journey alone. Hettie had been in touch with some friends of hers in Richmond and after dropping me at home, she would head there to visit them and spend the night, before returning home to Uncle tomorrow. Poor Uncle, how quiet everything would seem to him today with only Floss for company.

Floss, not understanding the difference between Hettie and I going down to the town and Hettie and I going up to London, was waiting expectantly by the car as she did every week when Uncle moved the vehicle out of the garage. She watched with interest, but without comprehension, as Uncle carried my suitcase out and placed it on the back seat of the car. It had been tacitly agreed that I would take only what I had come with, with the exception of my ant farm. The clothes that Hettie had bought for me would be of no use in the cold London weather that would be soon upon us, and by next summer, I would have outgrown them so they were really of no further use to me. Hettie had asked if I wanted to take Percy and I was sorely tempted to, but I thought that Uncle might have more need of him now. Hettie smiled and gave me a big hug when I explained this to her.

No longer afraid of Floss, I had no hesitation in going over to her and ruffling the fur around her ears, something I had discovered she enjoyed a lot. Her pink tongue lolled, her tail swayed back and forth, and her brown eyes looked longingly into mine.

My goodbye to Uncle was harder. Hettie had asked him to come up to London with us, but he had refused brusquely. He'd stated that London was not the place for him. I held out my hand to shake his.

'Thank you very much for having me,' I said formally as my mother had taught me to do. 'I've had the best time ever,' I added, the words coming straight from my heart. Uncle forced a smile and crouched down before me.

'I'm going to miss you,' he said very softly.

I threw my arms around his neck and held on as tightly as I could. 'I'll miss you too,' I whispered into the collar of his coat.

'Maybe you can come again next school holidays,' he suggested after I'd held onto him for some time with no sign of letting go.

'Could I?' I released my grip and stood back to look at Uncle directly in his bright blue eyes.

'I'll talk to Helen,' he promised. 'Here, give her some strawberries to get me into her good books,' he added handing me a punnet of freshly picked berries. Reluctantly, I accepted them and climbed into the front of the car, onto the seat next to Hettie.

My last view of Uncle that summer was that of an old man, with a scruffy bowl-cut hairstyle, wearing a long grey-white trench coat, and a lop-sided goatee waving forlornly as the car headed off down Stonebarrow Lane.

Chapter 7

That first weekend when I returned to my parent's house was the loneliest time I have ever known. Even now, I shudder to think of it. Before I ever went to stay with Uncle, I'd spent most of my time alone. Mother was always inside doing something, and I'd always been sent outside to play in the confines of our tiny, concrete backyard. I'd rarely been allowed to leave the boundaries of the yard, only permitted to venture out and play with the other boys and girls in our street when Mother stood chatting to their mothers; something she did not often do.

Prior to becoming ill, Father would mostly have been at work. If he was at home, he was often inside reading the weekend newspaper or tinkering with his model planes, something Mother forbade me to touch. Occasionally, Father would venture outside on a nice day and we'd kick the football around in our backyard. Sometimes, as a family, if weather permitted, we'd go for a walk to the park. Sometimes we'd have bigger outings, to the maze at Hampton Court or to the British Museum, but although I'd been there during these times, I was more of an added extra, not part of the main group. I was expected to tag along behind my parents or run ahead at a distance where I could still be seen, but not necessarily heard. Since Father had become ill, there had been no outings, no quick games of football in the ten-foot-by-ten-foot square that formed our domain. But although I'd mostly been alone in my life, I'd never actually felt lonely before.

Three months with Uncle as a constant companion, who was not just there, but who was actually with me, changed all that. I could now feel both alone and lonely. It was not just the lack of companionship that left me feeling bereft; it was also the loss of freedom that hurt as well. After months of roaming as far and wide as my legs would carry me, I was like a wild animal suddenly confined to a cage. Finding things to do in the open spaces of Charmouth had been easy, in my London backyard even my imagination felt stifled.

Hettie and I arrived in the middle of Friday afternoon. Mother opened the door in answer to our knock and said a simple hello to us both. She seemed neither pleased nor displeased to see me, in fact, for a minute I was not certain she knew who I was. Maybe after almost three months away, I looked different. Maybe she just had other things on her mind.

To me, Mother seemed unchanged, still the upright, slim figure wearing a plain dress under a floral apron. After giving her the strawberries and explaining they were from Uncle, we seemed unable to find any words to say to each other and for several moments, we three stood at an awkward impasse on the doorstep with no conversation and no action. Hettie finally took the initiative and stepped over the threshold and into the hallway. Mother had no choice but to close the door behind us.

'I'll take that,' said Mother in her tight clipped way, finally relieving Hettie of the burden of my suitcase.

'Thank you,' responded Hettie as Mother placed my suitcase at the bottom of the stairs. 'I'll say a quick hello to Gerald, if I may before I get on my way.'

Guessing where Father would be, I led the way along the corridor to the room at the back of the house. In the kitchen, Father, who had been seated in his armchair by the stove, struggled to his feet as we entered the room.

He also looked much the same as the last time I'd seen him; pale and thin, his breathing very raspy with the exertion of standing. I felt a glow of pleasure at the sight of him and I realised, belatedly, how much I had actually missed him. I moved over to stand beside him and he reached out a hand to affectionately ruffle my hair.

'Hello,' he rasped. 'It's good to see you.'

'You too, Father,' I beamed back at him.

He smiled at me fondly and then turned his attention to Hettie, greeting her warmly and thanking her for having had me to stay. The effort of this little speech left him breathless, the last of his words lost in the gasp for air.

Hettie took over the conversation, saying how much they'd loved having me, I'd been a breath of fresh air for them and they'd love to have me back again at any time. I looked hopefully towards both of my parents as Hettie said this, but they were not looking at me.

'Would you like a cup of tea?' Father asked.

'Hettie has to be going,' Mother said quickly. Father glared at her and nodded towards the sink. Obediently, Mother moved in that direction and began to fill the kettle with water.

'No thank you, Gerald,' Hettie interjected. 'Helen is right, I should probably get going or my friends will think I've got lost.' Mother replaced the kettle on the sink with a loud bang.

'Well, Joe,' said Hettie, turning to me and holding out her arms. 'Thank you for looking after Henry for me. It was so lovely to have you to stay and hopefully, we'll see you again soon.'

'Thank you for having me,' I responded with a loud sob as I wrapped my arms around her and smelt again that amazing aroma of baked goods.

'Don't worry, Joe, we'll stay in touch.' And with a final kiss on the top of my head, she was gone. Mother showed her to the door while Father and I stayed where we were. I quickly wiped away my tears so as not to make him think I was sad to be home. Father eased himself back into his chair with a look of relief on his face. He looked suddenly very pale and so much older than he actually was; almost as old as Uncle.

'Did you have a nice holiday, Lad?'

'Yes, thank you. Uncle and Hettie were very nice.'

'Told you you'd like him,' wheezed Father with a wink of his eye.

Mother appeared at the kitchen doorway with a frown of displeasure on her face at the sight of Father wheezing.

'You'd best go upstairs to unpack, Joe. Leave your father to rest. I'll be up in a moment to run your bath.'

'Yes, Mother.'

I turned reluctantly to go, wishing I had more time to spend with Father. There was so much I had to tell him. Father patted my arm reassuringly as I went past and I knew he understood; I would get to tell him everything, I just had to be patient.

I stood in the corridor outside the kitchen door for a moment searching for a feeling of being home. The house seemed stale and closed in, even though everything was neat and tidy and the place smelt antiseptically clean. I felt an intense longing for a hug from Hettie and for the bright blue eyes of Uncle to be resting on me as I studied the pictures of dinosaurs in his encyclopaedia. Behind me in the kitchen, I could hear my father softly admonishing my mother.

'What were you thinking, love, showing Hettie into the kitchen and not the front room? And you should have offered her a cup of tea.'

'I couldn't bring myself to be civil, Gerald, not after what she did to Uncle Henry.'

'You don't know she did anything to Henry. I think he was like that before, we just didn't know it. Besides, Henry seems happy now, surely that's all that matters?'

'Not in my book, it isn't.'

Not understanding what was being said I made my way quietly upstairs with my small suitcase and began to unpack my things.

൭൭൭൭൭

The start of the school year came as a relief to me. School was not what I expected it to be; I had pictured myself and the other kids in the class looking up things of interest in encyclopaedias, much like I'd done with Uncle. Instead, I found myself seated behind a desk spending my days practising writing the letters of the alphabet, which I already knew because Uncle had taught me, and reciting the times tables. It seemed repetitive and a little bit boring, but at least this was better than being confined to our concrete backyard.

During recess and lunchtime, I also got to play with other boys of my age, which was fun. My ability to make true friends was limited because I was not allowed to play with them after school as well. Mother expected me to go straight home, while some of the other boys had the freedom to stay out until it was their tea time. Still, I was included in their play during school breaks and never bullied like some of the other kids were. I knew from observing what went on that my lot could have been much worse.

Father continued to just sit in his armchair by the stove in the kitchen. As the months passed, his breathing worsened, becoming nothing more than a perpetual wheeze. It no longer required any exertion on his part for him to be gasping for air; just sitting in his chair was enough. When I got home from school, if Mother wasn't there, I'd sit in the kitchen with Father and tell him all of my adventures with Uncle in Charmouth. I described the beach and told him how Uncle and I had played Robinson Crusoe. I explained about the fossils we'd found and wished now that I'd bought some home to show him. I tried to draw pictures of what an ammonite looked like, but artwork was not my forte.

I gave mouth-watering descriptions of Hettie's baking, which Father said sounded delicious, but I wondered if it was there in front of him would he actually eat it. Father had no appetite. He ate very little, even less than I did. But his eyes shone with pleasure as I sat and talked to him and he seemed intent upon my every word during those stolen conversations we had. Mother had asked not one word about my time with Uncle.

One day, as we sat in the kitchen by the warmth of the stove, I mentioned to Father that Uncle had told me he was an organ.

'I think you mean an orphan,' wheezed Father with a smile on his lips. In as few words as possible, each one punctuated by a gasp for air, he told me how he'd been not much older than I was when the news had come about his father being killed at the front. His mother, distraught with grief, had refused to go to the air raid shelter that night. He'd been scared and tried to follow the neighbours to the shelter, but because they'd only just moved to that house, he didn't know them and didn't like to ask for help. In the morning, he'd followed them home again, unable to remember himself where his house was. The neighbour's house was still standing, minor damage only, but his home was a smoking ruin and there was no sign of his mother.

'Obviously killed by the bomb,' my father said philosophically twenty-two years later as we sat opposite each other.

'Do you remember them, what they looked like?' I asked. I'd had no problems remembering what my parents looked like, but I'd only been away for three months. I couldn't imagine what it would be like to have to store a picture of them in my mind for as long as Father had.

'Don't worry, Lad,' he said, ruffling my hair. 'You won't forget me. As long as you can picture us here together as we are now, it'll be alright, you'll see.'

At the time, I didn't know what he meant, but he was having so much trouble talking and breathing at the same time that I just let the subject drop.

๑๑๑๑๑

As promised, Uncle and Hettie stayed in touch. Where once Hettie had called every week so that I could talk to my parents, now she called every week so that I could talk to her and Uncle. Mother always answered the phone, but she never talked for long, quickly handing the receiver over to me with a pursed look of disapproval.

Hettie would talk to me first, every week she started by telling me how much Floss missed me. I was pleased about that and would picture Floss sitting by the phone as Hettie talked to me, her tail wagging and her pink tongue lolling out of her mouth. Then Hettie would ask how I was, how I was enjoying school, and what I'd been doing on the weekend. I always found that last question hard to answer because I'd been doing nothing. Hettie must have understood this, for after the first couple of calls she stopped asking that question.

Then I got to talk to Uncle and it was my turn to ask questions. I wanted to know if he'd found any more fossils. He said he hadn't, he wouldn't go looking again until I came to visit. This pleased me, made me feel that there was some hope of a return visit. I asked about our chickens; they were all doing well and had started to lay eggs on a regular basis. We spent several weeks discussing names for them, finally settling on Mrs Brown, Peggy, Gertie, and Willow. We also talked about the vegetable garden, I wanted to know what was growing now and what sort of chores Uncle had been doing there. If I mentioned something we'd been learning about at school, such as zebra starts with a z, Uncle would look it up in the encyclopaedia and report back on what he'd discovered in the next phone call. I became very knowledgeable on things beyond what I'd been taught in the classroom, but because of the week's wait for the information, the topic at school had changed before I could demonstrate my knowledge to the teacher.

I think of these phone calls as my lifeline during that year. The anticipation of them cheered me. I could spend my time alone thinking of things to tell Hettie and Uncle. Then, after the phone calls, I could spend days pondering everything I'd been told. I'd picture the garden full of winter vegetables and the henhouse full of eggs. I envisaged plates of Hettie's scones, piled high with jam and cream. I imagined myself peering over Uncle's shoulder as he looked up the origin of the alphabet in his encyclopaedia. In the midst of a life that consisted of school, the backyard and stolen moments with Father, that regular contact with Uncle and Hettie sustained me.

৶৶৶৶৶৶

Father's cough started as a single, dry clearing of his throat. I'd been home for months by then, Christmas had come and gone, and our routine afternoon chat, on the days that Mother was not there, was now well-established.

At the time, I didn't know where Mother went or what she was doing. The little I did know about her activities was that she always seemed to be ironing. Suddenly, great piles of sheets and shirts and dresses appeared and Mother stood in the kitchen ironing all day. Years later, I was to learn that Mother was taking in ironing as a means of earning some income. Father was no longer able to work and we had little money to live on. She went out to collect her loads of work in the morning, after I had gone to school, and then delivered them back, neatly pressed, in the evenings.

Father's illness was never mentioned in front of me. It was there all the time, the continual wheeze and gasping for air, but it was never referred to. Even now, I still have no idea what was wrong with him. Maybe it was lung cancer, maybe it was TB, it could have been emphysema, maybe it was something else entirely, I have no idea.

From the start of the school year, through Christmas and into March his condition didn't change much, at least not that I noticed. He did wheeze without exertion, but he still roused himself from bed every morning and still spent every day sitting in his armchair by the stove. To my young eyes that meant nothing had changed.

Then one day Father started to cough. Initially, it was like a clearing of the throat and occasionally he'd bring up a little bit of phlegm. Then the coughing spells grew more prolonged and more violent and the phlegm seemed to bubble constantly in his throat, like a pool of lava that was searching for the volcano opening.

The coughing fits frightened me. Father turned bright red and his face contorted with the pain of trying to clear his lungs of the mucous, while also wanting to fill them with air at the same time. He'd be left exhausted, with sweat pouring off him.

I hated to be left alone with him during those times. I had no idea what to do to help him and could only stand there mutely with a glass of water in my hand; the only comfort I knew how to offer. Eventually, it was not just phlegm that arose from his throat, but spots of blood that stained Father's handkerchief red.

One day, I was alone in the kitchen with Father, I'd just repeated a riddle I'd been told in the playground at school that day and had saved it in my memory to bring home to Father. I had wanted to cheer him up, he never seemed to smile much lately. He had chuckled at my riddle but that had brought on a particularly bad fit of coughing. Mother came in and found me standing there with my pathetic glass of water, while Father lay spent in his chair, his face still livid from the exertion, and blood spattering down the front of his shirt.

'Get out of here, Joe,' she screamed angrily. 'Can't you see that you are causing your father to cough?' She moved to shoo me out of the kitchen with a smack of her hand on my bottom, but Father's agitation stopped her.

'Leave him alone, love,' he wheezed at her when he finally had his breath back. 'We both know what's causing this cough and it sure as hell is not the lad. It'd be cruel to make him think he's responsible.'

It was shortly after this, that Father did not rise from his bed one morning. He was not in his armchair by the stove when I got home from school that afternoon nor in the days after that. From that point on, I'd sit with him in the bedroom, even if Mother was home. She never again said I wasn't allowed to. He'd lie in the bed, an ashen face against the white of the sheets.

He rarely talked anymore, just wheezed harshly while his chest rattled with fluid. So, I talked to him. I am not sure what I said, but I was careful not to pass on any more riddles. I do remember searching for memories of my stay in Charmouth that I had not yet relayed to him. Little things I'd forgotten to say, such as how Uncle almost lost our shoes in the long grass on the first day of our adventures together and how Floss had been the one to find them.

Early in May, one day while I was at school, the headmaster came to our classroom and asked for me. In the corridor, he told me that my father had passed away and that I needed to go home to my mother.

Chapter 8

I'd never faced death before, not even from a distance. With no extended family and no pets in my life, who was there to die? The finality of my father's passing eluded me for many months. The most immediate impact was for me to note, quite simply, how quiet the house was without his raspy breathing.

I didn't see my father's body; I was banished to the backyard when the undertakers attended our house. Maybe to have done so would have helped me to come to grips with what had happened, but either it wasn't the done thing in those days to expose children to the actual sight of death, or possibly my mother just didn't think it appropriate for me to lay eyes on a corpse. Whatever the reason, my father disappeared without me seeing him go.

Mother was sitting in the kitchen when I got home from school that day. Her eyes were red-rimmed from crying and her nose glowed like Rudolph's, but the rest of her face was pale to the point of being translucent. She did not cry in front of me. I never saw her shed a tear, nor did I ever see any evidence that she had been crying ever again. I didn't cry either, even though I was terribly scared and bewildered.

When Mother noticed me standing by the back door, she gestured for me to come over to her. At first, I thought I was in trouble for coming inside too early, but when I stood beside her chair as requested, she merely draped her arm around my shoulders and gave my arm a half-hearted squeeze. For a little while, we stayed like this, united by a common tragedy.

'Don't you worry, Joe, it'll be alright. We'll manage somehow.' And with that resolution made, Mother was on her feet and busy again.

The undertakers came and went. We had our tea; I was bathed and put to bed. The next morning, I arose to find my breakfast on the table as usual and Mother already sweeping the wooden floors. Apart from telling me I would not be going to school that day, there was no further communication between us. Father's passing was not mentioned. She did not go out to pick up her piles of ironing, instead, she spent the day thoroughly cleaning the front room, our best room, the one we rarely went into. I sat in the backyard, alone with my thoughts, feeling confused and abandoned by both parents.

Why had Father left us? Was life supposed to go on just the same as before when someone died? If it did, why would Mother need to find a way for us to manage somehow? What was there to manage? When would I go back to school? What should I be feeling right now? There was no one I could actually put these questions to, so I just let them tumble round and round in my head.

After that one, brief, shared moment with Mother, she appeared to have forgotten me. That evening as we ate our tea, I discovered that this was not the case.

'I've spoken to Uncle Henry. He said you could come and spend the summer with him again. You'll catch the bus down tomorrow morning like you did last time.'

Her voice was warm, kind almost, and as I think back on it now, I can see that like my first visit, this visit to Uncle had been arranged to shield me from the distress of coping with a situation in which I had a sick, and now deceased, father. It was never about banishment, but Mother never had the words, or the means, to explain that to me.

'Thank you, Mother,' I responded unable to hide my sense of relief and joy. Another summer with Uncle, freedom from the confines of our concrete backyard, Hettie's treats, and no tiptoeing around in fear that I would do something to displease Mother. It was the best news I could have hoped for.

Mother looked at me over the table, a sad sigh on her lips.

'You like Uncle Henry don't you?'

'Yes,' I enthused. 'He spends time with me, he's like my big brother, even though he's a very old adult.'

'Well,' she responded as her emotional shutters dropped back into place and the scorn and sternness returned to her voice. 'He's absolved himself from any form of adult responsibility, so I suppose he's got all the time in the world to play like a child.'

I didn't understand any of this, but I knew better than to ask.

The next morning, just like last time, Mother walked me to the bus station. She clasped my hand in one of hers and carried my suitcase in the other. This time, I made sure I used the toilet at the bus station, even though I had been before we left home.

The bus to Dartmoor left first and with the benefit of knowing what was happening to me, where I was going and why, I was feeling more relaxed and therefore more observant. I still felt that Dartmoor must be a nicer place than Charmouth because so many more people were going there. Knowing now that Charmouth was actually a fantastic place, I felt certain that Dartmoor must be paradise, but I've since learnt that things are not always what they seem. The thing that I did notice that day, and it puzzled me a lot, was why no one going there was carrying a suitcase like mine. Surely if it was that nice a place, you wouldn't just go for a day.

Mother stood well apart from all other passengers, standing tensely to attention. She did not relax at all until the Dartmoor bus had departed. Within minutes, my driver appeared, a jollier-looking man than the one I'd had previously. Again, Mother placed me in the front passenger seat, with my suitcase at my feet.

'Uncle Henry will meet you as before,' she said and with a kiss on my cheek, she was gone. There was no packet of sweets this time, but I didn't mind. Soon I'd be with Uncle and Hettie and that was a much better prospect than a packet of sweets.

ৡ৽ৡ৽ৡ৽ৡ৽ৡ

My reunion with Uncle was bittersweet. It was so wonderful to see him again, it was what I had longed for, but at the same time I knew that if Father hadn't passed away, this visit would not be happening.

When the bus pulled off the highway to take the road to Charmouth, I was lost in thought. I'd spent most of the journey trying to permanently imprint my father's image into my mind, I was so worried that I would soon forget what he looked like. I could still clearly picture the ashen face with hollow cheeks and sunken eyes propped against the white pillowcase. If I tried hard, I could even remember how Father had looked when he was sitting in his armchair. His facial features had not been so withered then and his skin had held more of a blue tinge, rather than the grey pallor of his last days. But it was hard for me to remember what he'd looked like before that, before he became ill, which was little more than a year ago now. If I could forget that quickly then Father's latest image would soon be totally lost to me.

The bus coming to a standstill surprised me. Roused from my reverie, I glanced out of the window and realised I was in familiar territory. The bus door opened and seconds later, Uncle's blue eyes were peering at me from under his mop of grey hair.

'Hello, Lad,' he said brightly.

'Hello, Uncle,' I responded, a little sob catching in the back of my throat, which I fought to suppress.

Reaching over the rail, Uncle retrieved my suitcase and together we stepped off the bus onto the side of the road. The door closed behind me and the bus roared away.

'Do you need to pee in the bushes again?'

'No,' I responded seriously. 'This time I went at the bus station before I got on the bus.'

'Wise move,' said Uncle with a nod of his head and an amused twinkle in his eye. 'Are you hungry? Hettie's made scones.'

I nodded shyly and reached up to place my hand in Uncle's free one. He looked surprised for a moment; I'd never before reached for his hand, but he clasped my fingers gently with his and together we set off along Stonebarrow Lane.

We didn't speak for a while and I used this time to look up and study Uncle. He was dressed much the same as the last time I saw him, wearing the same long coat, which now appeared a shade darker, no doubt due to ingrained dirt, for he never let Hettie wash it, no matter how often she pleaded to be allowed to. His hair was uncombed, as usual, but his goatee beard was neatly trimmed, and no longer lop-sided. Maybe Hettie had cut it this time. He still took long strides when he walked, at least two of my steps to every one of his, and it wasn't long before I was panting slightly.

'Hettie thinks we should send you to school,' Uncle said abruptly. 'You've got a few weeks to go until the end of the year and she's worried you might miss out on learning something.'

I didn't say anything for a moment. I didn't know what to say. I didn't want to go to school, I just wanted to be free with Uncle.

'Do you think I should go to school?' I asked tentatively, worried he might say yes.

'Gosh no! I think you learn more outside of the classroom than in it. I bet you were the only child in your class who knew what an Ichthyosaur was.'

I nodded because this was true. But some of the others in my class had been better at spelling and math than me and I admitted this to Uncle now because I knew that the teacher had thought that more important than knowing about long-extinct creatures.

'Humph,' grumbled Uncle. 'They've got their priorities wrong.'

We fell again into a companionable silence and continued our walk to the cottage. If Floss had been pleased to greet me as a perfect stranger, she was ecstatic to greet me this time as someone she knew but hadn't seen for a while. Her tail wagged furiously and she leaped and bounded around in front of me with such excitement. I had to tell her to sit three times before she calmed herself enough to obey. I reached out to scratch behind her ears, just as I knew she liked, and she almost melted into my arms, giving a sigh of pure contentment. Her body leaned heavily against mine as she looked adoringly at me with her big brown eyes.

Unlike last time, Hettie didn't hesitate to open her arms to me. As I moved into her embrace, I saw in her eyes that she understood the bittersweet nature of my return.

'It's so good to see you again, Joe,' she whispered into my ear. 'I'm so sorry about your father. Gerald was a lovely man, you must feel lost without him.'

This was my first, and only, condolence in relation to Father's death and it brought the tears flooding to my eyes and down my cheeks. Hettie's words made me understand that the feelings I'd been trying to suppress were valid feelings and that other people would understand them, I wasn't to be ashamed of them. With Hettie's permission, I allowed the distress, fear, confusion, and sadness I was feeling to escape from within. I don't know how long I cried on her shoulder but I do remember noting a significant wet patch there when I finally lifted my head again.

'I'm sorry,' I hiccoughed, trying to rub away the wetness with my hand.

'There's nothing to be sorry for,' she soothed. 'It's natural to cry when your father dies. Now we just have to balance that sadness out with a happy memory. Let's go and have a cup of tea and a scone and you can tell us one of your favourite memories about your father.'

With my face washed clean, I joined Uncle and Hettie in the kitchen. Over a cup of milky tea, with a scone piled high with jam and cream, I did as Hettie bade and talked about the time Father had kicked the football over our fence and in through the neighbour's window, which luckily was open. We all laughed at this and I felt how good it was to be home.

These four months with Uncle and Hettie acted as a buffer between the knowledge of my father's passing and the reality of it. In Stonebarrow Lane, I thought about my father every day, but he had never been a physical part of my life there and this shielded me from fully grasping that he would never be physically present in any part of my life again.

Uncle and I spent our time the same way we had last summer, we beach combed, went prospecting, worked in the garden and played whatever game came to mind. I could suggest anything and Uncle would always participate willingly. He never once said that he was too old for such childish games.

The subject of my attendance at school was resolved in our favour, although it did raise a "Henry, you're incorrigible" comment from Hettie. We only won the argument by promising Hettie that we would spend at least half an hour of each day doing some spelling and math, which we faithfully did. We looked at our natural surroundings to find words for me to spell. Seaweed, driftwood, farmer, chicken, house, beach, starfish, and ocean. These were the sorts of words Uncle would ask me to spell and if I stumbled, he'd help me until I got it right.

To practice my math, we'd collect shells from the beach and Uncle would propose a sum, such as four plus nine or thirteen minus eight and I would work out the answer and then check I had it right by counting the shells. Uncle also made me an abacus, which fascinated me. I'd spend some time every day shuffling the beads back and forth working out, what were for my age, quite complex calculations. Even after the school year finished and the holiday period began, we continued our daily lessons.

Of course, we still continued to consult the encyclopaedia, but my favourite reference book became the atlas. I loved to pick out a country and study its position in the world, its contours, whether it was landlocked or how many sea borders it had. I imagined what the coastline might look like, whether it was a sandy beach or steep cliffs and whether the land held mountains or plains. Uncle would help me look up more information in the encyclopaedia and I'd learn the name of the capital city, the national language, and the estimated population. Sometimes there were photos of a part of the country or of the people who lived there, I'd study these intently trying to picture myself amongst them. I especially liked islands and was slightly disenchanted to find that there were so few uninhabited islands left. My chances of an adventure like Robinson Crusoe's were slim.

This time, Hettie read us the story of *"Gulliver's Travels"* by Jonathon Swift. I was thrilled by his adventures of being a giant in Lilliput and a midget in Brobdingnag. My only disappointment with the story was that the places Gulliver travelled to were not real. I fully understood that *"Robinson Crusoe"* had been a story of fiction, just like *Gulliver's Travels*, but at least I could point to a map and think that might have been the island upon which Crusoe had been shipwrecked.

Uncle's energy never seemed to flag. He had seemed old to me the first time I met him and knowing now that he is 85 years old means he would have been around 62 years old that summer. He was always up before me and always on the go all day. He could walk for miles without ever seeming to tire, while I came home spent and often fell asleep on the couch before Hettie had finished our reading for the day. Maybe, though, my exhaustion stemmed more from me having to take two or three steps to every one of Uncle's. Whatever the cause, I certainly slept well every night, tucked up in my bed with Percy beside me.

Hettie and I also resumed our weekly shopping trips to Charmouth. The clothes from last summer no longer fitted me, for despite the stifling conditions of London I had managed to grow significantly over the winter months. I felt guilty about the money that was spent on me, thinking it not quite right, but Mother had only packed school clothes and Sunday best, neither of which were appropriate to the antics that Uncle and I got up to.

Uncle never came with us to the township, always claiming there'd be too many people there. He never asked me not to go, but he'd be slightly cranky on those mornings and was always pleased to have me returned to him.

Every week, just like last year, Hettie would call home. Of course, this time I only ever got to talk to Mother, there was no father there for me to converse with. Mostly, Mother seemed distracted, preoccupied with other issues. I understand now there were money worries for Mother to deal with, on top of her grieving for Father, but at the time, I thought that even from this distance; I had done something to displease her. I asked Uncle about it and he tried hard to come up with an answer, but I don't think even he could really explain it.

'Helen's always been a bit prickly,' he'd say or, 'she's just upset about your father, she'll come round again in time, you'll see.'

One day, we found a small hedgehog on the side of the road, not far from the cottage. It was alive but injured, Uncle said it had probably been hit by a car. It lay trembling as Uncle gently picked it up and it didn't try to fight us as we carried it home. Hettie found an old apple box and I collected dried grass and straw with which to make a bed for it to rest comfortably in. Uncle used an eyedropper to try and get it to drink some water, but the creature just looked at us warily through its tiny black eyes. We kept it in the kitchen by the warmth of the stove, but it did not rally and the next morning it died.

Uncle suggested that we bury the hedgehog in the garden. He dug a hole near the fence line while Hettie helped me make a cross from two sticks, which we painted white, and a bit of string. We kept the apple box as the coffin. Hettie, Floss, Uncle, and I stood at the graveside while Uncle said a few words about the hedgehog's life, thanked it for being a small part of our lives, and then mentioned how good it was that it would have no more suffering. Uncle said this was called a funeral service.

As we sat on top of Golden Cap later that afternoon, looking out to sea, I asked Uncle why Father hadn't had a funeral service.

'He did have one,' he told me. 'Everyone has a funeral when they die.'

'But, Uncle.'

'Yes, Joe.'

'Why didn't I get to go?'

'They don't let children go, which is silly really. You've got as much right to say goodbye as anyone, he was your father after all.'

'Can we have a funeral service for Father, like the one you did for the hedgehog?'

'If you'd like. But we have no body to bury, so maybe we should have a funeral where we send a wreath of flowers out to sea.'

I was pleased with this idea, but then a new thought occurred to me.

'Uncle.'

'Yes, Joe.'

'What happens to us when we die?'

'I don't know. Some people think the dead go to heaven where they can look down on all the people left behind. I don't really like that idea because I wouldn't really want someone I couldn't see watching everything I was doing. That could be a bit creepy, not a nice thought when you are sitting on the toilet.'

Even though I laughed at this comment, the image it conjured up in my mind made me hastily agree with Uncle's view.

'I think maybe nothing happens to a person when they die,' continued Uncle. 'Except that they die and all that is left of them is memories. Maybe heaven is a place in a person's heart, and rather than the dead person going there, we just keep a few memories of that person tucked away safely there. That way we can take the memories out any time we want and it's like that person is back with us again, if only just for a moment. Then we tuck them safely away again. But, Joe, you believe whatever gives you the most comfort because no one actually knows what happens, and therefore, what you choose to believe can't be wrong.'

I liked Uncle's idea of heaven, and unable to think of anything better myself, I decided to adopt it as my own.

ଓଓଓଓଓଓ

The following morning, Hettie helped me to make a wreath. We collected cuttings of green foliage, which Hettie wound into a circular shape, tied with bits of string here and there. Then we cut a variety of flowers from the plants in her flowerbeds and poked the stems through the foliage.

Uncle, Hettie, Floss, and I then made our way through the field of long grass, which had already been cut, along the cliff-top path and over the river Char to West Beach. This was the one and only time that Hettie ever joined Uncle and I on one of our outings.

We stood, barefoot, on the edge of the shore and Uncle asked me if I wanted to say a few words. I was holding the wreath high, not wanting it to hit the water until it was the right moment to let it go. I wasn't sure what to say at a funeral service so I demurred and let Uncle do the talking.

'We are gathered here today,' began Uncle in a soft but clear voice. 'To say goodbye to our dear friend, Gerald, husband of Helen and father of Joe. Although no longer with us physically, he will be forever in our hearts and will never be forgotten. Rest peacefully, Gerald, for you were a good man in your time.'

With a nod from Hettie, I bent forward and placed the wreath in the water that was lapping at my feet and gave it a gentle push. The wreath bobbed on the crest of a wave and for a moment, I thought it would be carried back past me and deposited on the beach. But the receding wave caught it up and carried it out towards the open water. Once we'd restrained Floss from chasing it, the wreath was soon able to drift, unimpeded, out to sea.

I watched it go and felt good that I'd been able to say my own sort of farewell to Father. Uncle and Hettie waited with me until the wreath was lost to sight and then we turned as one to head back to our home.

I noted as we crossed the mouth of the river Char how the flow of water had become little more than a trickle. Summer was drawing to an end and I felt certain that my return to London was probably imminent.

Chapter 9

When I did return to London, things were different. Mother looked thinner and had a white, pinched look to her face. But despite this hardening of her external self, she was actually a softer person on the inside. There were still times when she could be "prickly" as Uncle had called it, but these moments were the exception rather than the rule.

This change in Mother was probably most evident by the fact that I was allowed to be indoors with her. No longer did I have to wait outside until our tea was on the table. Mother welcomed me in when I got home from school, letting me sit in the kitchen while she got on with her ironing.

For the first few weeks, we were together in this way every day, but always in silence. Then, one day, Mother started to ask questions about my day at school. At first, I'd answer in short sentences, monosyllables, really. It was hard to talk to my mother; she'd never seemed interested in asking me anything about myself before. However, after a week or two, I started to open up a bit more, giving details about what we learned in school and sometimes branching off onto other subjects as well.

Eventually, I started to tell her about my time with Uncle and Hettie. I didn't tell her everything, there were some things I felt she wouldn't approve of, like us peeing in the bushes, and Uncle playing make-believe games with me. I was also cautious not to mention Hettie very often, for I knew there was something about Hettie that Mother didn't like. But I did tell her about our work in the garden, what the sea felt like on your bare toes, and how we'd read *"Robinson Crusoe"* and *"Gulliver's Travels"*.

Mother seemed most interested in my knowledge and skills in the garden, even suggesting that maybe we should plant some vegetables in our backyard. We never did do this though, simply because our backyard was all concrete; there was no dirt to plant anything in.

Mother didn't say much herself during these afternoon conversations, she just let me do most of the talking. I imagine she needed to fill in the silence, which seemed almost deafening without Father's raspy breathing as music to our ears. It made me realise how lonely Mother must have been when it had just been her here in the house while I was in Charmouth after Father's passing.

We never spoke of Father, just as his illness had been unmentionable, his passing was even more of a taboo topic. Really, we never seemed to speak of anything important. Certainly, our money worries were never mentioned. But even without being told that we had this problem, I knew it existed. There was less food on the table and sometimes only a meal for me and not one for Mother.

'I ate earlier,' she'd tell me, but I knew this wasn't true. I tried offering to share, but she'd shake her head and say she wasn't hungry anyway. It was hard trying to eat though, knowing Mother was going hungry, but wasting food was a serious crime in her eyes, so I couldn't risk her displeasure by leaving the meal untouched.

Mother was also reluctant to turn on the lights, or use the gas heating. She looked like she might cry when I mentioned that I'd outgrown my school shorts. My school shoes were also way too small for me, but after the reaction over my shorts, I thought it best not to say anything. It was not until she noticed me limping that Mother became aware of the problem. By then, my toes were almost deformed from having been cramped for weeks in those shoes.

While I was away in Charmouth, Mother had removed most of the evidence of my Father's existence. His coat no longer hung in the back porch, his razor was gone from the bathroom, and his slippers no longer poked out from under their bed. His model planes were all gone, and his toolbox no longer lived under the kitchen sink. I thought that Mother had thrown everything away, but I later discovered the toolbox in the back of the cupboard under the stairs. I presumed Mother thought the tools might come in handy one day and as a practical woman she wasn't going to throw them away permanently, she just wanted them out of sight.

It turns out she didn't throw the model planes away either, although she would never have classified them as potentially handy. These had been placed in a box in the attic, possibly put away for me in case I became interested in them when I was older. I only discovered them five years ago when Mother passed away from breast cancer and I was cleaning out the house prior to it being sold.

Two mementoes of Father did remain. One was a photo of him when he was a young man. It was encased in a silver frame and it sat on Mother's bedside table. I have it now, still in the same frame. It hangs on the wall in my lounge room, between a photo of Mother, taken just before her diagnosis when she still looked healthy, and one of me with Uncle and Hettie.

The other memento of Father was the armchair, it remained in the kitchen by the stove. Neither Mother nor I ever sat in it. I tried it one day, but it didn't feel right, sort of like I was sitting on a lap that wasn't there. Even Doug, when he moved in, avoided sitting there. After about two years, it was eventually moved to the spare room and I don't know where it went from there.

Our first Christmas without Father was very quiet. We'd never had big Christmas celebrations; that would have been a bit difficult when there was only ever the three of us. But we always had a special meal of roast chicken followed by plum pudding and custard. Father and I would get a Christmas cracker each and we'd wear the paper hats they contained while we ate our chicken and pudding. This year, Mother and I just ate ham and vegetables. The cuts of ham were real leg ham that Mother had bought from the butcher and I understood enough even at that age to know this was expensive and therefore a bit of a treat.

In previous years, I'd always received three presents: one from Mother, one from Father and one from Santa. This year there was only one present, from Santa. I could tell by the look and feel of the present that it was a book and this both intrigued and excited me. Santa had never given me a book before. I unwrapped it as slowly as possible, enjoying the anticipation. Inside the wrapping paper was the novel, *"Around the World in Eighty Days"*, by Jules Verne. This book has remained one of my most prized possessions ever.

'I told Santa that you seemed to like reading travel adventure stories,' Mother told me. I was so pleased with my present that I almost couldn't find the words to express it.

'Thank you,' I finally managed to say. 'It's perfect.'

The present created a dilemma for me: should I go ahead and read it by myself or should I save it to read with Uncle and Hettie over the summer? This was, of course, assuming I would be allowed to stay with them over the school holidays. Mother might not want me to go; she might be lonely here by herself.

I discussed this conundrum with Uncle over the phone. He assured me that it was a fantastic story, so good in fact that I should go ahead and read it. He said I would love it so much that I wouldn't mind hearing it again when I next stayed with them. He seemed so certain that I would be going to stay with them. I found this very comforting, although I did feel a pang of guilt that Mother would be left on her own again. Maybe Mother could come too, I thought. But I quickly dismissed that idea. I couldn't see it working out because Mother didn't like Hettie, and to be honest, she didn't really seem that impressed with Uncle either.

"Around the World in Eighty Days" was the best story I had read so far. It is still my favourite, one I have read many times over. I stumbled over some of the words as I read, and I didn't always understand everything (for example, what was a suttee?), but I grasped enough to know that this was a real story of adventure to real countries. I couldn't wait to view Uncle's atlas so that I could mark out the route Phileas Fogg and Passepartout had followed.

❧❧❧❧❧

A little after Christmas, our lives changed yet again. Mother got a job, not ironing at home, but a real job where she had to go to work every day. She was initially very flustered about the job; about being on time, about making sure she looked presentable, and about me being home alone after school.

During those first few weeks, things became very tense at home again and there were times when I felt that I preferred to have a mother who worried about money, rather than a mother who worried about her job. But we got through that period and things got better again.

I was seven and a half years old at this time and I was the only child I knew who came home to an empty house after school. It didn't bother me; I was never afraid, just sometimes a bit bored and lonely. I cured the boredom by trying to help out around the house. I would sweep the floors and set the table for tea. Mother would rush in, all flustered, and would stay tense and uptight until she had the tea on the table. By which time it would be late and I was pretty much sent straight to the bath and then to bed.

One day, I decided that if I prepared the vegetables, Mother would have less to do when she got home. I peeled some potatoes and carrots and put them in separate pots of water. I was careful when using the knife and was quite proud of my efforts. I left the pots on the sink as a surprise for Mother when she came home.

She was surprised and I think also pleased, but she never said so outright. She did suggest that I should put less water in each pot and that I should add a pinch of salt. From that point on, she would leave some potatoes on the sink each day, plus a plate of other vegetables in the fridge and I'd have them ready and waiting for her when she got home each night.

Our money worries didn't go away instantly like I thought they would now that Mother was working. She still sighed every time a bill arrived in the post, and she'd get that pinched look on her face. She worked as a sales assistant in a ladies' fashion shop. I know now that it wouldn't have paid very well, she probably earned less than half the salary Father had, and he was only a poorly paid tradesman. On top of our reduced income, there was also the debt she had incurred to pay for his funeral. However, Mother's job did mean that we ate slightly better, especially Mother who now shared every meal with me.

My school life was good. I found that I was better at spelling and math than the others in my class, so those daily lessons with Uncle had paid off. Hettie and Uncle called weekly and while I looked forward to their calls, it wasn't with the same desperation that I had awaited them each week last year. Mother and I were more comfortable with each other and while I was often alone, that suffocating sense of loneliness had left me. The only two downsides to my life were that I missed Father, and I didn't know if I'd be allowed to go to Charmouth again when the school year finished.

The advent of spring put a bounce back into Mother's step. The trees in the park displayed masses of pink and white blossom, and everywhere I looked there were yellow daffodils swaying in the breeze. The grey days seemed to be passing. Mother also brightened up her appearance with a splash of red lipstick on her lips. It made them stand out against the white of her skin and the black of her hair. She started to wear perfume again, a scent of violets that I remembered from when I was much younger. I can't remember when she stopped wearing it before, maybe it was when Father became ill and had difficulty breathing.

One fine Sunday in May, Mother suggested that we go for a walk in the park. We'd not been on an outing since before Father became ill and so I was terribly excited at the prospect. We didn't go to our local park like I thought we might. Instead, we caught a bus into the city and headed to Hyde Park.

Mother was wearing a pretty, white dress with a floral print and a light green cardigan that matched the colour of the foliage in her dress. She had applied her lipstick and a dusting of face powder. We strolled along together for a while until we reached the lake edge, where Mother pointed out some ducks splashing in the water. I was enchanted by these and Mother suggested that I go to the water's edge for a closer look. She would wait where she was, I could take as long as I liked.

I did as I was bid and was happy to discover six little ducklings swimming in the shallower water at the lake's edge. Careful not to get my clothes dirty, I knelt on the ground to get a closer look. They were butter yellow in colour and still covered in their downy feathers. I longed to pick one up and hold it but knew that I shouldn't, so I contented myself with watching them swim around trying to catch some of the bugs that landed on the surface of the water. Thinking Mother might find this amusing, I decided to see if I could entice her to come over.

She was talking to a man, who was dressed in a light grey suit and wearing a tie. Most other men in the park were more casually attired. Mother seemed slightly flustered, clutching her handbag tightly with one hand while patting her hair into place with the other. Despite the powder on her face, I could see a flush of colour rising up her neck and into her cheeks as I approached.

'Joe,' she said, reaching out to brush an imaginary speck of dust from my shoulder. 'This is Mr Harrison.'

'Hello, Mr Harrison,' I said, offering my hand as I'd seen Father do.

'Hello, Joe,' responded the man amicably. 'You've been admiring the ducks, I see.'

'Yes. There are ducklings, six of them. Do you want to come and see?'

I was really wanting Mother to come with me, but Mr Harrison assumed I'd meant him and so all three of us went to the water's edge to watch the ducklings play. After a few minutes, Mother and Mr Harrison seemed to tire of this activity and Mother suggested we continue our walk. Mr Harrison came too.

It was much like it had been with Father. The adults strolled ahead, talking to each other, while I tagged along behind. I didn't mind Mr Harrison; he seemed friendly enough, but I was confused as to who he was and why he was interrupting my outing with Mother.

At the far end of the park, Mr Harrison treated us to an ice cream. He and Mother sat on a wooden bench to eat theirs, while I stood on the grass behind them. I was very careful not to drip any ice cream onto my clothes. After that, we walked back through the park and Mr Harrison waited with us until our bus arrived. This whole time he only spoke to Mother, having nothing more to say to me. Apart from thanking him for the ice cream, I really had nothing to say to him either.

On the way home, Mother asked me if I'd had a nice day and I said I had, which was true. It had been a nice day, despite Mr Harrison monopolising Mother's attention.

'What a surprise to run into Mr Harrison like that,' she said, not looking me in the face.

The following weekend, Mother announced that Mr Harrison had offered to take us to High Tea at the Savoy Hotel. I was to be on my best behaviour, to mind my manners, eat with my mouth closed, and sip, not slurp, my tea. I was also to speak only when spoken to. I wasn't sure I wanted to go, not just because I'd have to be on my best behaviour, but because I'd rather have an outing with Mother alone, and because sitting down to a fancy tea in a posh hotel was not really the way I wanted to spend my time.

We arrived at the hotel to find Mr Harrison waiting for us. He was seated at a table for two. He rose to his feet as Mother and I approached, a look of surprise on his face.

'Ah, I see you bought Joe,' he said by way of a greeting.

'Yes,' responded Mother, looking slightly embarrassed and agitated. 'I...there is no...'

'It's not a problem, Helen, I don't mind,' he said politely, looking every bit like he did mind. Still, he summoned the waiter and asked for another chair to be bought to the table and we all took our seats. There was silence until a waiter appeared with a three-tiered plate of sandwiches, cakes, and pastries. Without asking what I might like, Mr Harrison gave me a cup of tea and a scone and then ignored me. The scone had a thin smear of jam and a dainty, piped, dot of cream on it. It did not taste anywhere near as good as Hettie's scones.

Mother and Mr Harrison began a stilted conversation while the tea was poured and treats were selected. They both seemed ill at ease and very nervous. Mother chose a cucumber sandwich and Mr Harrison ate just about everything else. They talked about the weather and about Birmingham, which is where Mr Harrison was from. They then moved onto a discussion on the cost of housing in London.

I don't know what was said after that. I took myself off in my mind on my own little adventure around the world in eighty days. Phileas Fogg had travelled by train, steamer, elephant, and sledge. He'd faced attacks by Indians, storms, separation from his travelling companion, and mutiny; all while being chased by a detective from Scotland Yard. I did all of that and more, adding in some daredevil flying stunts, cross-country skiing, and one-on-one combat with a wild tiger. I was in the process of climbing out of an ice crevice with the help of some husky dogs when Mother got to her feet.

'Thank you for the tea, Mr Harrison,' I said, also rising to my feet. He nodded at me but didn't respond.

'Yes, thank you, Doug. It was very kind of you to invite us. We've had a lovely time.'

'It was my pleasure, Helen. Maybe next time we could…' Mr Harrison didn't finish his sentence, just made a little gesture towards me with his hand. It was the sort of gesture Mother made when she was shooing me out of her way.

'That's a little difficult, Doug,' Mother responded with sad, downcast eyes.

'Oh well. Never mind then,' he said and Mother suddenly looked very sad.

This time Mother didn't ask me if I'd enjoyed myself, which if I was honest I'd have to say I hadn't.

The following weekend, there was no invitation and no outing. Mother and I stayed home alone. Mother seemed a little put out by this but I didn't mind. I had other things to worry about. There were only four days left of the school year and nothing had been said about a visit to Uncle. I was trying to get the courage up to ask Mother about it, even though she wasn't in the best of moods when the phone rang. It was Hettie with an invitation for me to come for all or part of the summer. She and Uncle knew that Mother had to work, and had thought that might be causing her some upset to have to leave a seven-year-old boy at home alone every day.

Mother readily accepted the invitation and it was settled that I would travel down by bus the following Friday.

I was relieved to know that I'd see Uncle and Hettie again soon. I felt slightly guilty about leaving Mother by herself. But I couldn't help but wonder if Mr Harrison hadn't waved at me dismissively like that, would Mother have agreed to let me go?

Chapter 10

Even at age seven and a half, I felt the difference between London and Charmouth, our house and Uncle's. Despite the improvement in my relationship with Mother, there was still an overwhelming sense of escape, of the easing of tensions, as I returned to Stonebarrow Lane. Here, I felt that I could breathe deeply and properly. I was like a snake that had shed its skin and was now able to move unhindered by any type of constriction. If London was my reality, then Charmouth was my fantasy; a dream life come true.

Uncle, Hettie, and Floss were all enthusiastic in their greeting. Percy was waiting for me, propped up against the pillows on my bed, just as I had left him. Mrs Brown, Peggy, Gertie, and Willow all clucked with glee when I approached them on the first morning to collect their eggs from beneath them. Chores awaited me in the garden and adventure lay just beyond the back gate.

The weather that summer was perfect. Uncle shed his long coat, which seemed to be getting greyer by the year, rolled up his trouser legs and waded out into the sea to help me learn how to swim. He never wore a bathing costume or went swimming himself, but he happily stood mid-thigh in the sea and gave words of encouragement as I splashed past him doing a very rudimentary dog paddle.

That was also the first year that Uncle and I had a night time adventure. I knew nothing of Uncle's plans, I'm not even sure if Uncle ever made any plans or if our adventures were always a spur-of-the-moment thing. I was asleep, curled up in an exhausted heap with Percy lost under the blankets beside me when Uncle's soft voice brought me to a groggy state of wakefulness.

'Joe. Joe, are you awake?'

I'm not sure that I responded verbally, just rolled over and peered in the direction of the doorway with half-closed eyelids.

'It's a nice clear night tonight. A good one for gazing at the stars.'

Uncle's whispered voice wafted over to me and the power of his suggestion brought me finally fully awake. I slid out of bed and scrambled into my clothes. Quietly, I made my way past the open door to the bedroom where Hettie lay sleeping. Her gentle, purring snore blended in with the sound of the crickets chirping out in the garden. At the back door, I found that Uncle had already put his socks and shoes on and was sliding his long arms into the sleeves of his coat. I hastily followed suit.

Without making a sound, we let ourselves out of the back door. As if from nowhere, Floss suddenly appeared at our sides. One of the hens started to cluck in consternation as we walked past, but Uncle whispered for it to be quiet and go back to sleep. It obeyed.

The moon was not quite a quarter full, providing barely enough light for us to see by. Cautiously we made our way across the field of long grass to the top of the cliffs where we could hear the waves gently lapping on the beach below us. Here, Uncle lay down on the ground and cast his eyes skyward.

'There, Joe, that group of stars is a constellation called Pegasus, the winged horse.'

I lay down beside Uncle, and Floss flopped at our feet. Looking up to where he was pointing I could easily find a group of stars, but try as I might, I couldn't make them into the shape of a horse. I didn't tell Uncle this, in case he was disappointed in me, so he went on to point out the constellations of Aries and Pisces. We gazed in companionable silence for a few moments.

'Uncle.'

'Yes, Joe.'

'Can we see Leo?' This was my star sign and I was anxious to spot it in the hopes that I could make out the shape of the lion, but Uncle said it was too late in the year for it to be visible. I'd need to look skyward in spring.

Uncle then went on to point out Ursa Major and Ursa Minor, which he told me were also known as Great Bear and Little Bear. Uncle was in the process of telling me that Little Bear represented Ida, a nursemaid who'd looked after baby Zeus so that his father, Cronus, wouldn't swallow him, when I fell asleep.

I awoke as the sun was rising above the horizon, stiff from lying on the hard ground and slightly damp from a sea mist that had rolled in during the night. Uncle, still lying beside me, also stirred in the early morning light. Floss was already up, off fossicking in the long grass. Wearily, we trudged home to be greeted by a frantic Hettie, who very firmly told Uncle that he'd been more than incorrigible this time.

That adventure, one we repeated several times more that summer, left me with a slight head cold and an ongoing interest in mythology. It did not awaken any interest in astronomy, for I could never make any group of stars into the picture of a horse, bear, or any sign of the Zodiac.

True to Uncle's word, we did read *"Around the World in 80 Days"*. As predicted, I found lots of extra details in the story this second time around. I also finally learnt what a suttee was, although I must admit the thought of it left me cold. In Uncle's great atlas, I traced the journey of Phileas Fogg and his companions; thrilled to be able to trace a real adventure through real countries.

'I'm going to do that journey one day,' I told Uncle. His response surprised me.

'Why would you want to do that? You can already see the whole world from here.'

This was the first inkling I had that maybe Uncle's spirit of adventure did not extend beyond his own backyard.

All too soon, the summer was at an end and I was on my way back to London, to Mother, to yet another year at school, and to a surprise that I hadn't anticipated.

Throughout my stay in Charmouth, Hettie had, as usual, made a weekly phone call to Mother. I'd been torn between my desire to tell Mother everything I'd been doing, just like we'd started to do at home, and my guilt at leaving her alone. However, the warmth I'd felt from her over the past year seemed to be absent over the phone.

I assumed this was because she was alone and spending her days working, while I was with Uncle and Hettie and having a wonderful time. This intensified my guilt and made me feel bad that I had not only left her but had wanted to be here rather than there. It turns out that Mother was not home alone that summer, Mr Harrison had become a lodger in our house. There had been a point to his conversation about the cost of housing in London after all.

Mr Harrison was given my room as his own. I was moved to the spare room, which is so small that it had never been used as a room, just a storage space. My bed fitted along one wall, but it took up so much of the available space that the door was not able to fully open and I had to squeeze through it.

I didn't mind that I'd had to give up my room. I didn't mind that my new room was tiny. I didn't really mind Mr Harrison living in our house. The only thing I did mind was that my relationship with my mother had gone back to the way it used to be before Father died. I was to be seen and not heard, and even then, I should be seen as little as possible.

During the weekdays, Mother and Mr Harrison went to work. Mother still had her job in the shop. Taking in a lodger had further eased, but not solved, our financial situation. I went to school, where I had lots of acquaintances to mingle with, but no close friends. After school, I came home and swept the floors, laid the table and prepared the vegetables just as I had done the year before. Mother came home and cooked a quick meal and we all three ate in silence. After we'd eaten, Mother did the dishes, Mr Harrison read the paper, and I did my homework. I struggled with some of the math and science questions but I stopped asking for help after Mr Harrison told Mother that I must be a bit of a slow leaner not to know some of the things I had asked about.

Mr Harrison didn't speak to me directly, except to tell me to do something or fetch something for him. Mother told me that he was a paying guest and therefore I should do as he asked. I wouldn't have minded if only he had asked, not ordered.

On the weekends, Mother cleaned the house, Mr Harrison read the paper, and I took myself out into our concrete backyard. On Sundays, Mr Harrison would go out, but even without him being in the house Mother didn't talk to me the way she did before. Occasionally, Mr Harrison asked Mother to go with him. She always seemed pleased to be invited along and hurried to put on her best dress and some lipstick. I was never included in the outings.

My solace was in the books that I read. Now that I was in grade three, I was allowed to borrow books from the school library. The librarian was at first sceptical about the nature and number of books that I borrowed, but through our conversations, I convinced her that I was a good reader and that I did actually read every book from cover to cover. She began recommending books for me to read, and so I expanded my reading genre beyond stories of travel adventure.

I talked to Uncle and Hettie every week. Again, they were my lifeline, the reminder that for some small part of the year, I had a dream life somewhere else that was vastly different from my real life in London.

At Christmas, Mr Harrison went home to Birmingham for a week. Mother was quiet and sad during that time and our Christmas was not a happy one. Part of me had hoped that it might be like it had been the previous year when it was just the two of us. But deep within me, I knew that I was only a child and could never be the type of companion that Mother wanted. Even when I became an adult, Mother and I were never able to recapture the sort of relationship we'd had for barely one short year.

As the summer school holidays approached, Mother announced that she and Mr Harrison were to be married. They would be going on a short honeymoon to Brighton. I would be going to spend the summer with Uncle and Hettie as usual. I would not be at the wedding; they could see no point in delaying my departure for Charmouth just for that. Mr Harrison's only comment on the marriage was to say that I should call him Doug from now on.

I was uncertain how I felt about Mother remarrying, but I decided not to dwell on it. Instead, I went to Charmouth and had a wonderful time with Uncle and Hettie, repeating old adventures and adding a few new experiences to my collection. That summer Hettie read us David Copperfield by Charles Dickens. It reassured me that as far as step-fathers go, Mr Harrison, that is Doug, was not as bad as he could have been.

Chapter 11

There were only two changes in my life when I returned to London. Firstly, I had my old room back, Doug now having moved into Mother's room, and secondly, the photo of my father now sat on my bedside table rather than on Mother's. Otherwise, our lives were unchanged. Mother and Doug went to work and I went to school. On Sundays, Doug and sometimes Mother would go on an outing. I went nowhere. Neither Mother nor Doug tended to speak to me much, except to tell me what to do.

There were times when I felt despair when I missed my father and wished he hadn't died. I knew that Mother would still be the same as she was now, but at least I'd have Father to call me Lad, and kick the football with me. In those moments, I thought of David Copperfield or Oliver Twist (Hettie was making her way through a few of Dickens's novels) and I knew then that I had nothing really to be sad about.

In the summer months, I had my reprieve: three months with Uncle and Hettie. After Mother married Doug, it became a matter of routine for me to spend every summer holiday in Charmouth, while they went to Brighton for a fortnight. I don't know if this was at Doug's insistence because he wanted a break from me, or if Mother just thought it was for the best. Whatever the reason, I was happy with the arrangement.

Our routine in Charmouth was largely unchanged too. Uncle and I, together with Floss, wandered the hills and beaches. We went prospecting and beachcombing. We nurtured the garden, cared for the chooks, and got into as many escapades as possible, such as falling into the River Char fully clothed, and getting lost in the sea fog, almost walking off the top of the cliff. Hettie would greet us most days with a "Henry, you're incorrigible", which I think Uncle just loved to hear.

Hettie and I went weekly into the township to do the shopping and have morning tea. Hettie also joined the local library so that I could borrow books on

Greek and Roman mythology, something that had really captured my imagination. Despite my considerable reading ability (I was already tackling *"War and Peace"* by Leo Tolstoy by the time I was twelve), Hettie continued to read to Uncle and I most evenings. *"Animal Farm"* by George Orwell, *"A Farewell to Arms"* by Ernest Hemingway, and *"The Woman in White"* by Wilkie Collins were just a few of the novels she read to us over the years.

I didn't notice Uncle and Hettie getting any older. They had looked old to me from my very first visit and I think they just stayed that way. Floss grew older and slower and eventually, she found it too hard and too tiring to spend a whole day fossicking with Uncle and me. The fact that I could finally keep pace with Uncle's stride I attributed to my growing bigger and stronger, not Uncle growing older and slower.

His mind remained sharp, he seemed to know so much more than I would ever be able to learn. I asked him so many questions over the years, everything from how the earth was formed, to the economic laws of supply and demand. When I was thirteen, having suddenly developed an interest in such matters, I even asked him how to strike up a conversation with girls.

'You know, Lad,' he responded. 'I'm not really sure.'

I liked the way that Uncle was always honest with me. If he didn't know the answer he said so, if I'd asked a factual question we solved the problem by looking it up in the encyclopaedia. When it was a question of this nature, he would tell me what he knew or thought, and then leave it to me to work it out from there.

'What I remember from my time as a young man was not thinking of them as girls, but just as people. That way I could speak to them just like they were anyone else. The only difference would be that girls like compliments. Boys don't need to hear that their hair looks nice, but girls do, so you need to remember to say that every now and then.'

It was sage advice that I have remembered to this day.

The summer I turned fourteen was the ninth summer I stayed with Uncle and Hettie. It was not the same as the summers before.

It started well enough, Uncle met the bus as usual. He carried my case, even though I was well and truly capable of doing that myself. I easily kept pace with his long strides and this made me pleased to think we were now on equal footing. Floss rose stiffly to her feet and came slowly down from the porch to greet me. She was still pleased to see me, but too old now to show it as enthusiastically as she had before.

I hadn't seen my father age before he died, so until this moment I'd never really formed the link between the two processes. But in watching Floss move so slowly and painfully, it finally struck me that she probably wouldn't be around for much longer, that things in Stonebarrow Lane were not constant as I had always thought them to be, they could, and would, actually change.

Hettie embraced me warmly and then stepped back, patted her bun back into place and looked me over, commenting on how much I had grown. With a jolt, I realised this was true, I was taller than Hettie now, almost as tall as Uncle. The house, Uncle, Hettie, the garden, and my room were all unchanged, except that everything seemed smaller and somehow constrained. Percy was sitting on my bed and I picked him up to give him a quick hug. I felt slightly embarrassed to do this at my age, and as if to demonstrate how grown-up I was, I moved him from my bed to the chair under the window. Hettie had baked scones, I ate four of them, piled high with jam and cream. My mug of tea was strong and tasty, made with only a drop of milk now.

That evening we played cards, which is what we routinely did on my first night in Charmouth. Uncle had wanted to play Snap as usual, but Hettie suggested that it was probably time they taught me to play Rummy and Gin Rummy. Uncle relented, but reluctantly. I was pleased with Hettie's suggestion because I felt that as well as growing physically I was also growing mentally and my mind had gone beyond Snap; I needed something more challenging.

The following morning, Uncle woke me early as was the usual practice, but I was reluctant to rouse myself from my bed. Over the last few months in London, I'd taken to lying in later and later on the weekend mornings. Not because I was necessarily tired and needed to sleep, but just because I was a teenager. On this morning, however, I could have definitely slept longer so I was probably feeling slightly grumpy even before Uncle suggested that we play Robinson Crusoe. I didn't mind going beachcombing, but a part of me recoiled at Uncle still referring to it as playing Robinson Crusoe. This had been fine when I was five, even when I was ten, but I was older now. If I was too old to "play" anymore, then definitely so was Uncle.

'I'd like to go beachcombing with you, Uncle,' I responded sleepily, with an emphasis on the word beachcombing. 'But can we go later after I've had a bit more sleep?'

Uncle seemed put out. It was almost like his bottom lip lowered itself into a sulk, but he said nothing, just padded across the hallway to his bedroom.

'Joe doesn't want to get up yet,' I heard him say petulantly to Hettie.

'That's not surprising, Henry, it is very early,' was Hettie's sleepy response. 'Come back to bed, leave the lad to re-energise his batteries. He's doing a lot of growing lately, he just needs some extra sleep. You can go to the beach later.'

Over the next few days, Uncle would suggest that we "play" at being Saxons or archaeologists or palaeontologists. I bristled every time, couldn't he see that I had become too old to play childish games now? It seemed to me that I'd grown and matured and Uncle hadn't. He was more childlike than I was, but in an adult like him, that childlike quality just made him seem slightly…well crazy or mad.

I hated myself for thinking this. Just last year when I returned to London after my summer holiday, Doug had asked me about Uncle. It was one of the very few times that Doug actually spoke to me other than to issue an order.

'So how mad is he then, this Uncle Henry of yours?' he asked as we sat at the kitchen table. 'Helen says he's as nutty as a fruit cake.'

I was so offended and outraged by the question that I got up and left the kitchen without a word. Now here I was thinking the exact same thing myself.

Uncle didn't wake me again after that, he always waited until I'd dragged myself out of bed. Every morning, I found him waiting anxiously for me in the kitchen, and then there'd be another delay before we could head out while I ate my breakfast, Uncle having long since finished his. I felt guilty, but I also felt resentment, like this wasn't my fault, it was Uncle who was making me feel this way because he didn't seem to notice that I had grown up and so should he.

That summer I went along with all of the activities that Uncle suggested. I still enjoyed them, I just didn't want to call them a game. Even so, my favourite times with Uncle were the times we worked companionably in the garden and the times we sat on Golden Cap and I plagued him with questions.

'Uncle.'

'Yes, Joe.'

'How does an engine work?'

'When will men land on Mars?'

'What is the Vietnam war all about?'

I could talk to Uncle about anything; anything except my desire to tread in the footsteps of Phileas Fogg and travel around the world in 80 days.

'You can travel via books, just use your mind. You don't need to actually go to these places,' he'd tell me.

'But I want to see them in real life, and to actually experience being there,' I tried to explain.

'But what you see in your mind might be better than the reality. If you go somewhere and it doesn't live up to your expectations, then you'll end up being disappointed.'

I didn't understand what he meant then, but I did years later when I stood surrounded by the slums and poverty of India. Although the practice of suttee had always repelled me by its barbaric nature, India was still one of the countries I most wanted to visit. I had conjured up an image in my mind of turbaned men, and sari-clad women, all brightly coloured, riding on elephants through exotic jungles. The reality was so far removed from this image that, as Uncle predicted, I was very disappointed and vowed never to return to India again.

But I loved Spain, San Francisco, and Hong Kong, and even though Phileas Fogg had not ventured in this direction, I went to Yosemite National Park and thought it one of the most beautiful places on earth.

꙰꙰꙰꙰꙰

The following year, my tenth with Uncle and Hettie, I was even less content with the summer break in Charmouth. In fact, I hadn't even been sure I really wanted to go, and so it was with some reluctance and reservation that I boarded the bus in London for the four-hour bus trip. I loved seeing Hettie and I still really enjoyed spending time with Uncle, but after going beachcombing and prospecting once, I was not overly enthusiastic about doing it again. The novelty had well and truly worn off; I was a bit bored with it now. I also felt a yearning to step beyond the boundaries that I had lived within for so long, so I suggested a trip to Portland or Pinhay Bay. Even Lyme Regis would have been something different.

Uncle went strangely quiet when I made this suggestion and Hettie looked momentarily flustered.

'We could go if you like, Joe, just you and me, but Henry doesn't travel very well, so he might prefer to stay at home.'

Uncle said nothing, he just looked sad and lonely, bereft almost, like he'd lost something precious. Later, I overheard him with Hettie asking why I didn't want to play with him anymore. I felt awful and told Hettie it was alright, we didn't need to have an outing. But I struggled to put aside the adult I felt I'd become and slip back into the child Uncle wanted me to be.

As I lay in bed that night, I pondered the mystery that was Uncle. It occurred to me that Uncle never left Charmouth, in fact, he didn't even really go to Charmouth because in all the years I'd visited, he'd never once been into the township. He'd never come to London with Hettie and I on the few occasions that Hettie had driven me home at the end of the summer. He'd never been on holidays. His life was restricted to a distance of no more than five square miles. Uncle might let his mind wander to distant places, but there were physical boundaries that Uncle never crossed. This realisation troubled me and I began to ponder a few of Uncle's other "eccentricities", as Father had called them.

The clothes he wore hadn't changed in all the years I'd been here. He had no friends, never seemed to talk to anyone other than me and Hettie, and occasionally, Mother. He refused to have a television, saying it polluted the mind. He played like a child, even though he was an adult. His behaviour and his antics had all been fun for me when I was a child, but when I looked at him now with my almost-adult eyes, I found I was no longer comfortable around him. 'Mad Uncle Henry' Mother had called him and with my limited knowledge of madness, this label perturbed me.

A few days later, while we wandered the beach, I noticed a group of local youths, two girls and three boys, sitting at the shore's edge. I'd seen them before when I went into the township with Hettie. They usually hung around in the high street, but I'd also seen them boarding the bus to Portland, obviously going on an outing for the day. At the time, I'd envied them this opportunity. I'd also envied them their friendships, their shared lives and experiences. I had a small group of acquaintances, but no one you'd really call a close friend. For the majority of my life, my best friend had been a man almost sixty years older than me.

The girls were lying on towels, soaking up the sun's rays. They had stripped down to their bikinis and behind their sunglasses were pretending to be unaware of the three boys ogling them, sitting on the sand nearby. The boys, for their part, couldn't keep their eyes off the girls, which was understandable because neither could I. They were slim and curvy at the same time, and I'd never seen so much bare female flesh on display before. Uncle seemed not to notice the group as he walked past them with his head down intent on fossicking for shells.

I lost the little interest I had in this activity and surreptitiously focussed my attention on the group of youths as I walked past them. I longed to be part of them, to be part of any group really, not specifically this one. I let Uncle get several yards ahead of me, trying to make it seem like we were not together, but the boys were not fooled.

'Glad I'm not stuck spending the summer with me old grandad,' I heard one of them say loudly. 'He's a bit nutty, but not as nutty as that old weirdo.'

As we returned along the beach, the group had risen to their feet and were kicking a football between them. The girls had pretty hopeless ball skills; they were more intent on flashing their bodies and giggling at the boys. One boy, too focused on watching the girls, failed to stop the ball as it came towards him. It sailed past him, straight in my direction. I deftly kicked it back towards him. He kicked it back to me and for a few moments we exchanged kicks and I felt like I was part of a group of my contemporaries. As I moved nearer, the boy spoke to me, 'What's with the old guy? Is he trying to take off Catweazele?'

My face flushed crimson as a mixture of embarrassment and shame washed over me.

'No,' I managed to respond. 'He's just eccentric.'

'He's not eccentric,' one of the girls sneered. 'He's madder than the Mad Hatter and all the guests at his tea party put together.'

With my head down, I scurried past, the sound of their laughter ringing out behind me. After that experience, I was reluctant to go anywhere in public with Uncle. I felt ashamed of my attitude, but I also felt ashamed to be seen with him. I made excuses: there were things to do in the garden, I didn't feel well, Hettie needed my help, it was too hot, too cold, too wet. Anything I could think of. Hettie noticed and asked me if everything was alright. Uncle noticed and just looked at me sadly, occasionally going off on his own.

The summer ended and for the first time ever, it was a relief to go back to London.

Chapter 12

After that summer, I decided I would not return to Charmouth the following year. Instead, I would get a job, earn some money and then the following summer, after my last year of school, I would take off on my adventure around the world. I started with a part-time job, working after school restocking shelves in the nearby supermarket. This would increase to at least three full-day shifts during the summer holidays. It was tedious work, with no thinking required. To relieve the boredom and keep my focus on why I was doing this, I let myself daydream about the travel adventures I would have. This way, I managed to get through my shifts every week.

I delayed telling Uncle and Hettie about my plans; I didn't want to upset them any earlier than I had to. We still spoke on the phone every week and because I still enjoyed talking to Uncle, it was only being seen with him that was embarrassing, this contact was easy, it made me feel like our bond was still there.

It was during one of these weekly calls that Uncle told me Floss, aged fifteen years, had died. She'd just slipped away peacefully in her sleep. He cried as he told me and as upset as I was at the loss of Floss; I was uncomfortable to hear a grown man cry. I'd never seen my father cry, and Doug was certainly not the sort of man to ever shed a tear.

Uncle and Hettie tried for many months to live without a dog, but eventually, they could stand it no more and Jess came into their lives. This happened around the Easter break at school and I put aside my reservations about going to Charmouth and slipped down for that week to meet the new puppy. She was beautiful; with soft, fluffy black and white fur, and a very mischievous and playful nature. Luckily for me, the weather was dreadful and apart from quick, short walks with Jess, we did not venture out at all. This meant I did not have to think of ways to avoid being seen with Uncle in public.

On the last day of my stay, I took the opportunity to let Uncle and Hettie know of my plans for working over the summer. Uncle looked crestfallen, and while Hettie seemed distressed, she put on a brave face and tried to be supportive of my plans.

'That's a wonderful idea, Joe,' she said nervously trying to pat her bird's nest bun into some sort of shape, while also darting anxious glances in Uncle's direction. Uncle said nothing, just turned away.

That summer was tedious. It was hard enough to get through twelve hours a week packing shelves, but to do it for twenty-four was almost unbearable. I found myself even longing for the repetition of the summer holiday activities with Uncle. But it was a good experience in that it helped to strengthen my resolve to go to university. I did not want to end up as a labourer like my father, or as a shoe salesman like Doug.

This goal, and my status as a part-time worker, gave me a feeling of superiority. Not just over Doug and, I'm ashamed to admit, my own father for their lowly, menial occupations, but also over Uncle. I'd gown-up and Uncle hadn't. I was going to be a professional: to work in a position of responsibility, unlike Uncle, who'd stayed a child all his life and had never been accountable or responsible for anything or to anyone.

During this last year at school, I focussed only on school work and on planning my big adventure. Feeling guilty about abandoning Uncle and Hettie, and also because I missed their companionship, I returned to Charmouth for the Easter break again. Just like the previous year, we were mostly confined indoors by the weather so the visit was without tension on my part.

I chose not to talk to Uncle and Hettie about my travel plans, I knew they upset Uncle but I couldn't understand why. I did think of asking Hettie about it, but concluded that it was probably part of Uncle's "madness" and it would, therefore, be an uncomfortable question for her to answer. It did cross my mind that maybe Uncle was opposed to me travelling because he wanted to contain me, to keep me childlike so that he would always have someone to "play" with.

However, the Easter break with them turned out to be a lovely experience because our time together was mostly taken up with reading, either novels or the encyclopaedia, and this served to emphasise Uncle's intelligent side rather than his mad one.

With my final exams completed and my application to study law at City University accepted, I headed off around the world.

My journey was a fantastic experience. There were so many new and wonderful things that I got to see and experience; the richness and variety of life around the world was, and still is, a source of wonder to me. I found myself wishing often that Uncle could be there to share the experiences with me. I know that he would have marvelled at the beauty of Yosemite. He would have loved the steep inclines in the streets of San Francisco, and possibly even have challenged me to a race to the top. He would have shaken his head with bemusement at the way of life in Hong Kong where so many people lived stacked on top of each other, crowded in towering apartment blocks, but he wouldn't have felt disappointed by what he saw there. Of course, I saw sights that disappointed me, and I saw sights that upset me. But I believe that I grew from those experiences, and despite Uncle's misgivings, I would rather have seen them than not.

Upon my return to England, I had another brief visit to Charmouth, were despite his earlier derision of my plans, Uncle turned out to be the most avid listener to all of my travel stories. At first, I only told him of the good things I had seen, but eventually, I mentioned how confronting I had found the slums of India. He looked concerned as I said this, and then asked me if I was alright, had this upset me too much?.

'I'm fine, Uncle,' I replied. 'It was difficult to witness, but in a way, it was necessary to see it, to help me understand how lucky I am to live here and to have the way of life and the opportunities that I do have. I'm good, Uncle. It's okay.'

I think Uncle felt a sense of relief to know that I had grown from my travel experiences, rather than become bitter and disillusioned, for I heard him confess to Hettie some hours later that my journey had been a positive experience for me after all.

With eighty days of travel behind me, I headed off to university and the next phase in my life.

༄༄༄༄༄

I fitted in with my contemporaries at university in a way I never had before. Unlike at school, where everyone went because they had to, the students here were mostly enrolled because they wanted to be. Finally, I had some peers of my own age who shared my interests. I remained a relatively serious and studious young man, but I also allowed myself to party, and to indulge myself in newfound friendships.

I had chosen to study law because I wanted a career where I could feel that I was helping others. But about half-way through my first year, it dawned on me that I would mostly be helping people after they had fallen into trouble. It would be like shutting the stable door after the horse had bolted. What I wanted was to prevent the trouble from occurring in the first place, so I switched the focus of my degree to sociology and ended up with a Bachelor of Criminology and Sociology. To this end, I now work with the Government as a Criminologist, trying to understand what drives crime in our society and how best to put in place policies to lower crime rates and prevent recidivism.

When I explained my change of focus from law to sociology over the phone, Uncle seemed extremely distressed about it. He became incoherent in his distress and I could not understand what the upset was all about. Despite my recent positive encounters with him, the "Mad Uncle Henry" tag sprang again to the forefront of my brain. Finally, Hettie took the phone from him and said she would call me back later when she had calmed him down. She did call later and reassured me that Uncle was okay. She then very politely, and apologetically, without any explanation, requested that I did not mention the subject to Uncle again. I didn't bother to find out why, I just assumed it was another of Uncle's eccentricities and was simply happy to comply.

Just like his acceptance of my need to travel, albeit after the fact when he had seen that it did me no harm, Uncle did eventually accept the career I had chosen. He talks about it with me now, every time I visit or when we speak on the phone, and he follows the research part of my role with great interest. I am glad of this, but question why I had to go through the trauma of his initial reaction to eventually reach this outcome.

During my four years at university (I added on an extra year to complete my masters), I only made sporadic visits to Charmouth; staying no longer than two to three days. Our phone calls also became less frequent, for I was often too busy with study or my social life to make the call. At some point though, I do remember noticing that Uncle and Hettie were getting older. Uncle seemed less sprightly than he had been and Hettie was going greyer.

Two years after I finished my degree, I met Clara and a year later; we were married. I invited Uncle and Hettie to the wedding. I didn't expect Uncle to attend, but I felt certain that Hettie would be there. Surprisingly she sent her apologies, saying that she wouldn't be able to leave Uncle alone overnight. I thought this an odd excuse because she had certainly done so many times before, staying with her friends in Richmond after she had dropped me home, but when Clara and I went to visit on our return from our honeymoon, we discovered that Uncle had suffered a minor stroke.

Physically he'd suffered no impediment, but he had a few cognitive issues, mainly a total loss of the concept of time. He would want to get up during the night and head off for a walk with Jess, he'd expect his afternoon tea at breakfast time, and occasionally, he'd put himself to bed at lunchtime and sleep through most of the rest of the day. For a man who'd had an uncanny ability to know exactly what time it was without reference to a clock, this impairment was particularly disturbing.

About this time, Doug suffered a massive heart attack and died three days later in the hospital. I did not mourn his passing personally, he had never been an important, or even likeable person in my life, but I did wonder how Mother would cope, having had two husbands pre-decease her. She seemed to fall to pieces slightly, becoming more querulous than usual and complaining constantly of one discomfort or another. In the end, this turned out not to be due to Doug's passing. A few months after his death, Mother was diagnosed with advanced breast cancer which had spread to her spine and lungs.

We had never managed to regain the rapport we shared briefly in that first year after my father's death. I was distressed to see her months of suffering, but her passing did not leave me with as much of a sense of loss as Father's had. Maybe this was due to my being so young when Father died, or maybe it was because of the difference in my relationship with each of my parents.

While I was distracted by these events, Uncle began to show signs of dementia. He couldn't remember the name of the lane he lived in. He was often forgetful, letting the bath run over and leaving the back gate open so that Jess would escape into the field of long grass. He could not always participate in conversations, sometimes not understanding what was being talked about and therefore making comments that were out of context and absurd. I remember once him saying that he couldn't breathe because the air was taken up with rays from the microwave.

This part of the disease distressed me the most. As far as I was concerned, Uncle had always known everything. His mind, which had always seemed sharp, became a bit soft and out of focus. He did, however, finally seem to accept that I was a grown man now, and no longer wanted to "play" when I came to visit.

He did not forget people. He knew who Hettie was and who I was, but he often forgot that we had Jess now and frequently referred to the dog as Floss. He could never grasp who Clara was, though. I guess she'd appeared after the disease had started to take hold, before he'd had a chance to lock her into his memory.

Hettie refused all offers of help and refused to consider Uncle moving to live in a nursing home, stating firmly that she believed it would kill him. They'd manage just fine she told me. I was relieved that little was required of me, except for the occasional visit and the odd phone call. I didn't like to see Uncle this way; it was too close to madness, something I had never wanted Uncle to be. So, I did not visit as frequently as I should have. I got on with my life and let Uncle and Hettie stay isolated in theirs. Then the phone rang and it was Hettie asking for me to help with the unthinkable.

Part 2

Chapter 13

It is a shock to see Hettie. Uncle looks much the same, his hair is thinner and he has a slight stoop, but he still has the same wiry physique, his goatee beard, and piercingly clear, blue eyes. Hettie has shrunk. Her hair has also thinned, she looks pale and tired and her eyes appear dull; they have lost their merry sparkle. She has lost weight and, for the first time since I met her, is thinner than Uncle. I feel such a sense of guilt. I have been only too pleased to know Hettie had total responsibility for caring for Uncle and I didn't have to lift a finger, but I never stopped to consider the toll it might be taking on her.

She embraces me warmly and I catch a faint whiff of freshly baked goods hidden beneath the more pervasive smell of old age. She ushers me into the kitchen where tea and scones await. Uncle dances around like a young child, he is so excited to see me. I presume this to be one of his better days; his mind seems quite lucid.

'I'm sorry about the scones, Joe. I was going to make some sandwiches for our lunch, but Henry insisted that you'd want scones as soon as you arrived.'

'Of course, he'd want scones. Joe loves scones, they're his favourite.'

'I've found it easier to give in rather than try and fight him once he has his mind set,' Hettie adds as an aside to me.

'You never have to apologise for your scones, Hettie. Uncle is right, they are my favourite.'

I say this sincerely, for ever since my first day here, my mouth has watered at the thought of Hettie's scones and today they don't disappoint. Uncle and I help ourselves, both eating four scones each. Hettie has one and then only picks at that. For the amount of food Uncle can consume, I wonder why he hasn't grown fat. Evidently, dementia has not slowed him down physically and possibly, Hettie has become thin from all her running after him.

We eat scones, drink tea, and catch up with the news. Uncle and Hettie, who go nowhere and do nothing, have very little to tell me. I wonder again how they can stand this life. I suppose they have no choice now, with the dementia that plagues Uncle, but to me, it seems they wasted so many years stagnating here in Charmouth when they could have been off doing all sorts of things. I fill up an hour telling them about my work and activities in London. Uncle alternatively drifts off to his own world and then comes back to participate lucidly in the conversation. Hettie asks how Clara is and Uncle asks who Clara is.

After we've finished eating, I go upstairs to my old room to freshen up and unpack. It has been many years since I last stayed overnight, having made only day trips to visit since Uncle was diagnosed with dementia. My room hasn't changed. Nothing in this cottage has changed, except Uncle and Hettie. My single bed looks so small and I wonder if I'll still fit into it. Percy is sitting propped up against the pillows and I feel a sob rise to my throat to see him there. Like Uncle, he was such a good friend to me in my childhood and now, I've grown up and left them both behind. I pick him up and place his beak against my nose, capturing again the furry softness and fresh smell from when I first held him close as a lonely boy of five. I think Hettie must have washed him, for I'm sure he should have the smell and feel of my chubby, dirty little boy fingers all over him, but he doesn't.

Closing my eyes, I let the memories of my childhood come flooding back. I can picture the lost and frightened boy that I was on that first visit here. With a rush of images, I experience everything again that Uncle and Hettie did to make me feel welcomed and loved. I think of the amazing bond that developed between Uncle and me. I know that somewhere in my teens I lost what we had, but even though I could no longer feel it, I never forgot it. I miss the way things were, but I can't go back to being a child again and I am here now to totally bury what once was. Hettie obviously can't go on like this, it is blatantly obvious that Uncle has to go to a nursing home.

It occurs to me, thinking of the state Hettie is in, that perhaps she too plans to go into the home. Maybe that's why she has finally managed to make the decision that she has, having always been adamant that Henry would never leave her care. I will not discuss the nursing home situation in front of Uncle. I have no wish to distress him and I doubt that Hettie has mentioned anything to him, but I resolve to talk to Hettie about it at the earliest opportunity.

I make my way back downstairs, passing Uncle on his way up.

'Goodnight, Joe. Sleep well,' he tells me.

'But, Uncle, it's not even three in the afternoon yet.'

'Early to bed, early to rise, makes a man healthy, wealthy, and wise,' is Uncle's response as he continues up the stairs.

'Uncle's gone to bed,' I tell Hettie when I meet her coming out of the front room to look for him.

'I'll go and check if he's alright,' she responds, leaving me to make myself comfortable.

The front room is another part of the cottage that has not changed. The table where I had my first afternoon tea still sits under the window. We have never eaten there again, but we have spent many evenings seated around it playing cards. I browse through the bookshelf, spotting all the books that Hettie read to us during the long summer evenings. The nostalgia is overwhelming and I feel the tears well up in my eyes again.

'You loved those stories didn't you?' Hettie comes up quietly behind me.

'These were the best times of my childhood, my summers here with you and Uncle.' I respond, rapidly brushing the tears away before turning around. 'Where is Uncle by the way, surely, he's not really going to bed now?'

'He's already settled himself into bed and I imagine he'll go to sleep for a while.'

'But if he sleeps now he won't sleep tonight.'

'It's irrelevant what happens now in terms of what will happen later. Henry could sleep now and not sleep later, or he could not sleep now and still not sleep later.' Hettie gives me a wry smile and shrugs her shoulders as though to suggest it makes no difference to her either way, but I can see the exhaustion in her expression. I reach out to give her a quick hug.

'Has it been really bad?'

'It's been okay, challenging, but okay.'

'I should have come. I should have helped more, but I really had no idea what you were faced with.'

'It's okay, Joe. This is not your problem. Henry is not your responsibility. I've only asked for your help now because I can't go and look at the nursing homes and leave Henry on his own.'

'Uncle doesn't have to be my responsibility for me to help. When I think of how much you and Uncle did for me when I was young, I wasn't your responsibility then either, but you still helped me.'

'Oh Joe,' responds Hettie patting me on the arm. 'You really don't know that you gave much more to Henry than we ever gave to you.'

'Did I?' Hettie's comment surprises me. I can't envisage how I could possibly have given anything to Uncle. All I can see of myself, as I look back, is a lonely boy, then a sulky, albeit confused, teenager, and now a self-centred young man.

'Did you never realise how lost Henry was when you went back to London each year?'

'I don't think I realised, or even knew, much about anything to do with Uncle.'

'No? I did always wonder what your mother told you about Henry, and about me, but I was never game to ask.'

'Nothing about you, I'm sorry to say. I didn't even know that you existed until Uncle told me when we were halfway along Stonebarrow Lane on my first visit here. Mother didn't say anything about Uncle either. Not directly to me anyway, but I did overhear her referring to him as Mad Uncle Henry.'

'Did Henry ever say anything about his past?'

'No never. And I never asked, which is amazing really because I plagued him with a million other questions over the years.'

Hettie laughs at this.

'Sit down, Joe, I'll tell you Henry's story now. It's important that you know.'

We both take our seats, me on the lounge where I always sat with Uncle, and Hettie in the armchair that was her usual seat. Hettie fusses for a moment, adjusting the cushion behind her back, trying to get comfortable. I wonder briefly if she is procrastinating but quickly dismiss that idea. That's not in Hettie's nature, both she and Uncle have always been straightforward and honest with me. But then Hettie cocks her head to the side as though listening for something and I start to wonder again.

'Was that the front door?'

I focus my hearing in that direction, trying to capture any sound, but I hear nothing.

'I don't think so.'

'Oh.' Hettie looks perplexed. 'I thought I heard the latch.'

'Would you like me to go and check?'

At first, I think Hettie will refuse my offer and get up and do it herself. But tiredness seems to overcome her and with a sigh, she nods ascent.

I make my way into the hall. The front door looks closed from this angle, but to fully allay all of Hettie's fears I go over to check. I find the door pulled to, but not shut. I pull it open but there is no one on the doorstep, not even Jess and I know this to be her favourite resting spot. I put my head out of the door and check both directions up and down Stonebarrow Lane.

A light drizzle has started to fall and the overcast conditions this late on a winter's day have made it quite gloomy. Even so, I can clearly see the pale, naked, figure of Uncle striding rapidly up the lane in the direction of the intersection with The Street. I step onto the porch and call his name, but he appears not to hear me.

Quickly, I make my way through the kitchen to the backdoor, where Uncle's coat hangs on the coat peg. It is the same coat he has worn for these last twenty years and more; now threadbare and shabby and of an indistinguishable colour. I imagine, even with his fuddled mind, he is still refusing to let Hettie wash it, let alone throw it out and get a new one.

Grabbing the coat, I go back to the front door. Hettie, aroused by my call, stands on the front porch looking with dismay at the sight of Uncle's retreating figure.

'Go and run him a hot bath,' I tell her. 'He'll need warming up after this escapade. I'll go and fetch him back.'

As I step into the lane through the open front gate, I can make out Jess's black and white body trotting faithfully after her master. I can only hope that she'll follow him home just as faithfully because I won't be able to go dashing off after her as well.

I increase my pace to a rapid trot and set off after Uncle. I try calling his name again, but he doesn't hear me. Uncle's pace is quite remarkable for a man of his age, but I feel that he is slowing a little and I think he seems to have started shivering. I gain on him and call his name again.

This time he hears me, but my voice startles him and he steps rapidly off the sealed section and onto the earthen verge of the road. The rain has made the ground muddy and slippery and he loses his footing, falling heavily to the ground. I cover the last few yards to him at a sprinter's pace.

'Uncle, are you alright?'

Kneeling beside him, I check for obvious signs of injury. There are none, but he is covered in mud, grass, and grit from the ground and I am sure he'll have a graze and a bruise or two under all of that. He is also very wet and his skin feels icy cold to the touch. He looks so shrunken right now, like a cold, wet, over-large child with wrinkly skin. He is shivering uncontrollably. I try to ignore the fact that I am touching Uncle's naked body, something I have never seen before, let alone touched. Putting his coat around his shoulders, I assist him to his feet. He is compliant and unresisting.

'Come on, let's get you home. Hettie will be worried,' I tell him. 'Where were you going, anyway?'

'I have to meet the bus. Joe is coming so I have to meet the bus.' His teeth chatter as he tries to speak and his shivering has become quite violent.

'But I'm here already, Uncle. I drove down this morning in the car. We had scones when I got here, don't you remember?'

'Ah, so you are here. It is wonderful to see you, Joe. Did we really have scones? They're my favourite you know, I'm sure I'd remember if I'd had my favourite scones today.'

'Yes, we really had scones. They were delicious, the best Hettie has ever made. There are some left, so why don't we get you home and cleaned up and then you can have a hot cup of tea and another couple of scones to eat.'

'I would like that.'

Uncle walks along beside me, limping slightly, without complaint. I have my arm around his shoulder and my other hand is holding the coat closed around him as best as I can. I feel awkward, both physically and mentally, in this process of assisting Uncle. I try to imagine how uncomfortable Uncle might have felt on that first day I arrived when he had to pee in the bushes so that I would too, but surely doing things like that would have been easier for him because he was the adult and I was the child. Now it seems like our roles have reversed, but he is not a child and at the moment, I don't feel very much like an adult. Jess trots along faithfully at Uncle's heels. On the front porch, Hettie waits for us, a pinched anxious look on her face.

'Look who's here,' Uncle calls out excitedly. 'I've just met Joe off the bus.'

Hettie helps Uncle into the bath while I go into the kitchen to put the kettle on. I hunt through the pantry and find a couple of leftover scones. These I put into the oven to warm. I'd offered to help with the bathing but Hettie said she'd manage. Uncle is capable of climbing in and out of the bath himself and supervision is all that is required from her.

I feel quite shaken, almost physically ill, from the incident. I have barely spent four hours in Uncle's company and already I'm feeling stressed. How ever has Hettie coped by herself, day in and day out, for all of this time? I hope that the wandering and nakedness are only recent phases of Uncle's illness. Certainly, Hettie hasn't mentioned incidents like this occurring before. But it is now apparent that Hettie hasn't really been telling me all that has been going on.

I hear Hettie and Uncle coming downstairs so I pour the tea and take the scones into the front room. Uncle is seated in his usual spot on the lounge, warmly dressed in his pyjamas and dressing gown and in this outfit, he looks really old; frail almost.

'Do you think I should ring the doctor?' I ask Hettie.

'No. Henry has a few scrapes and bruises, nothing broken. I've put disinfectant on the wounds and wrapped up the worst graze on his arm. I think they'll be fine.'

'I was thinking more about the exposure to cold factor, it could lead to pneumonia.'

'Oh. Yes, of course.' Hettie looks uncertain for a moment and then comes rapidly to a decision. 'Let's leave him for the moment, if he has a temperature in the morning we'll call the doctor then.'

I nod in agreement and place the tray with the scones and Uncle's mug of tea onto his lap. His face lights up with pleasure. Hettie looks slightly disapprovingly at this double helping of cream in one day.

'Sorry,' I say to her. 'I did promise him, though.'

'It doesn't matter,' she says with a resigned sigh, taking her seat. 'High cholesterol is really the last of our worries.'

I offer her a mug of tea and then take my seat next to Uncle, balancing my mug of tea on my knee.

'Shall I read a chapter, Henry?' asks Hettie.

'Yes please,' responds Uncle licking a dollop of cream from his finger before turning to me. 'We're reading "*Watership Down*" by Richard Adams. Hazel and Pipkin have just rescued some hutch-bound rabbits from Nuthanger Farm.'

Hettie looks surprised and I assume, correctly as it turns out, that Uncle's account of their place in the story is accurate. Picking up the book and her glasses from the table beside her armchair, she commences to read.

"*Watership Down*" is not a story I was am familiar with, but this does not matter. I just love hearing the sound of Hettie's voice. She has always been exceptionally good at pacing the story through the way that she speaks and changing the tone and lilt of her voice depending on which character is speaking.

Before the chapter is finished, Uncle is asleep, his head tipped back and his mouth open. He is snoring slightly. I gently remove the tray from his lap and place it on the floor at my feet. He does not stir. Hettie finishes the chapter and replaces the book and her glasses on the table. Together, we contemplate Uncle.

'He looks so sweet and innocent when he's asleep,' she comments. 'So much more childlike.'

'He's always been childlike, as far as I'm concerned. Old, but still childlike.'

'Has he? Well maybe, but you didn't know him before.'

'Before what?'

'Before…No, let me start the story at the beginning, Joe. You need to be able to see Henry as he was to help you understand what happened to him and why.'

Chapter 14

Uncle's story, as Hettie relays it, is that Uncle was forty-nine years old and she was thirty-seven when they met in 1951. Hettie had just started working in Uncle's faculty: the London School of Economics and Political Science at the University of London.

'I was a secretary and Henry was a genius,' she tells me and for a moment, the sparkle returns to her eye.

Uncle had a doctorate in economics as well as a degree in social welfare, but it was his economic skills that the university was interested in. He was tenured as a professor; he could have been a dean, but Uncle wasn't interested in hierarchical achievements.

This news astounds me on two fronts. Firstly, I have never doubted Uncle's intelligence. Right from the beginning, I thought he was a man who knew everything. But I'd never considered the possibility that Uncle had ever held such a high academic position or that he had completed a doctorate. I have never really even contemplated the notion of Uncle having a job before. The other thing that astounds me is that Uncle has a degree in social welfare.

'But,' I say to Hettie, shaking my head in disbelief. 'Uncle was so upset when I told him I was changing from law to sociology and social welfare. Why would that upset him if it was something he'd done himself?'

'I'll get to that Joe, but basically, it was because he worried that you'd experience the same pitfalls, the disappointments, and stresses that he had.'

Resuming her story, Hettie goes on to tell me that Henry had been a young teenager during World War 1, not old enough to go to war, but old enough to see its impact. His family had been reasonably well off at the start of the war and while they'd suffered some losses, not the least of which being the death of Henry's father, my great-grandfather, they were still fairly comfortable at war's end. Not everyone was so lucky. Hettie goes on to explain in some detail what society was like at that time.

There had been a lot of casualties from the war and also from the Spanish Flu that swept the world in 1918. A lot of families had lost their breadwinner. Unemployment was high, as was inflation. Women, who had joined the paid workforce in large numbers during the war, had been employed for the duration of the war only. As the men came home, the women were expected to hand over the jobs to them. This was alright if you were lucky enough to be in the situation where you had a man who came home and who could find a job. But only just alright. With rising inflation and a falling demand for British exports, the future was not looking good.

Some women could still work, but only if there was no returned serviceman wanting the job. Of course, the wages paid to women were very much lower. Preference in employment was given to widows and single women. So, families where the husband couldn't find work, or where he couldn't work due to war injuries, suffered. Even a widow who could find work wasn't always able to take the job if she had young children. The nurseries that had sprung up to support working women during the war all closed down once peace came again. Some widows, facing no other option, took the job at miserable wage rates and left their children home alone. It was that or starve.

All of this troubled Uncle, but he didn't feel that he was the sort of person who could have a direct role in addressing the problem. His response though, was to study economics. He aimed initially to work with the government in setting fiscal policy that would stimulate the economy and thus provide prosperity for everyone.

'Henry was both sensitive and idealistic from the start,' Hettie tells me. 'Not like his sister, Alice. Her response to the plight of those around her was to marry a man from a "good" family with lots of money, even though she didn't really like him that much. I'm led to believe maybe that's why Alice was so hard on your mother for marrying your father. Gerald had neither money nor an understanding of his family.

'Your uncle was committed to his cause, to the point that a degree in economics was not sufficient,' Hettie goes on to tell me. 'He went on to get his master's and a doctorate, just to ensure that he had sufficient knowledge to tackle the problem. He also travelled widely to investigate economic policies and their impact on other countries.'

'Uncle travelled?' I am so astounded by this news. My picture of Uncle, which cracked at the start of Hettie's story, has now shattered completely.

'Of course.'

'But he was so against me going abroad.'

'Henry has only ever wanted to spare you his bad experiences, Joe. You'll understand this when I finish the story.'

I try to keep quiet so that Hettie can continue with her explanation.

While overseas, Uncle saw lots of things that upset him. Not just poverty and unsanitary living conditions, but also inhuman treatment and subversion of the masses, just so that a few select people could hold all of the wealth in their hands. Uncle wanted to believe that the world was a good place but he saw too much to convince him that it was not. His response to this was to stop travelling, to withdraw himself from being faced with disappointment.

'It was not about burying his head in the sand, Henry wasn't the sort to think that if he didn't see it then it didn't, couldn't, exist. Henry pulled away because he didn't know how to deal with it, he didn't know how to fix it,' Hettie explains.

I'm perplexed by Hettie's words at first, for Uncle had always seemed to have an answer to everything I asked him. But, I reflect, my questions as a child were all of a nature where an answer could be found in the encyclopaedia. True, I asked questions about death and talking to girls, but I'd never touched on the subject of social inequality, never really touched on my interest in the area, or explained the reason why I had chosen law and then switched to sociology. I don't delve into any of that now either, just let Hettie continue.

As per his plan, Uncle worked for the British Government, developing economic policy. But he felt he had little input, a lot of decisions were made that disappointed him. In 1925, Churchill restored the pound sterling to its pre-war exchange rate. This made British exports too expensive. Industry attempted to redress the issue by cutting costs. The major cost was labour, therefore, wages were cut. Then the Great Depression hit in the early 1930s and unemployment rose dramatically.

According to Hettie, it was the everyday impact of these things that troubled Uncle; what it meant for the average working man on the street. The problem with economics and fiscal policy, Uncle thought, was that everything was expressed as a statistic, the cost of living has risen by three per cent, or average household incomes are down by twenty per cent. But what did that actually mean?

'Statistics don't explain the human impact and that impact is so variable that "average" is meaningless,' Hettie tells me. 'For some households, a fall of twenty per cent in income might mean that they can't afford a holiday or a new car this year. For others, that drop means that there is one meal less on the table each day, or children go to school without shoes and warm jumpers. That's what worried Henry the most,' she explains.

In response to this problem, Uncle became a student again, he studied social welfare in the hopes of better understanding the issue and relaying them to the government. The government wasn't interested, they preferred the statistics to the reality.

Then World War 2 started. Uncle tried to enlist; he didn't agree with war, but he still felt he should do his bit for his country. However, Uncle was never a practical hands-on type of man, and he was thirty-seven by then so he was not considered for active duty. He was, however, given a role in the war finance department. This went against the grain for Uncle; to be part of wasting money on a process that was about killing people while letting those who were alive live so poorly. But it was wartime and he really wasn't able to do anything other than what he was told. If he tried, he risked being labelled unpatriotic, even treasonous.

It was after the war that he went to work at the University of London. He'd never married, he'd just dedicated his whole life to trying to get the reality, not just the facts, considered in economic decision-making.

As well as lecturing and supervising several PhD students, Uncle was conducting research on the impact of various economic models. The aim of his research was to find a means to accurately measure the impact of government policy, giving consideration to all variables, but expressing it in human terms not just statistics. He wanted no more talk of a three per cent rise in unemployment; with the people affected by this remaining anonymous people somewhere out in the suburbs away from politician's eyes. Uncle wanted to be able to express this impact in more defined human terms by naming the industries and professions that would be directly affected as well as the places where they lived, the impact on their health, their children's lives and their prospects for the future. The work was quite advanced when Hettie joined the team.

'He was the nicest boss I'd ever worked for,' says Hettie. 'On my first day, he showed me around the department himself. He introduced me to the rest of the team. He told me I was to call him Henry, not Professor, and then he said that my hairstyle really suited me.'

Hettie reaches up to pat his bun back into shape as she tells me this. I have a chuckle to myself remembering Uncle's advice given to me as a young lad on how to talk to women.

Henry, she relays, worked long hours and Hettie, also unmarried and with no other family commitments, often stayed late to help.

'I'm not an intellectual like Henry, but I'm no dummy either, so Henry could talk to me about his research and I understood. More importantly, I also understood his passion to include a real picture of the impact on the everyday family. My father had been a lost person, part of those statistics on so many occasions.'

Despite the tiredness written all over Hettie's face, a flush of energy and passion had washed over her as she talked about Uncle's beliefs. This quickly fades into resignation and finally, sadness as she starts to tell me about her family.

Hettie's father was a shipbuilder in the East End of London. He went off to fight in World War 1 just a month after Hettie was born. Although left with no ongoing physical disabilities as a result of the war, her father was psychologically scarred by the experience. He was one of the many thousands of men who returned from the war to reclaim their old jobs but were unable to reclaim their old lives.

Initially, he was one of the percentage of men who found employment, then he soon became one of the percentage of men who turned to alcohol to dull what they'd seen and done at the front. This, in turn, led to him becoming one of the percentage of men who were laid off following the downturn in the shipbuilding industry, which was due to the high cost of exports from England, which in turn was due to the over-inflated value of the pound sterling. Eventually, he became one of the percentage of men who couldn't cope and took their own lives.

The flow-on effect, she explains, was that Hettie had to leave school to look after her younger brother and sister, both of whom were much younger than her having been born post-war. Their mother went out to work to support the family, earning a pittance and ruining her health in the bargain.

After the younger children were grown up, and their mother had passed on, Hettie had gone into domestic service, having no qualifications for anything else. It was during World War 2 when so many women were required for clerical roles, that she had the opportunity to gain her secretarial qualifications and skills, which eventually led to her working with Uncle.

After a year of working together, she says matter-of-factly, Uncle asked Hettie out to dinner and two months later they married.

'We shocked a lot of people. Not just because of the age difference and the stigma of the boss marrying the secretary, there was also the fact that our families and friends had long ago confined us to the categories of bachelor and spinster. Then there was also the speed of the wedding. I think a lot of people expected me to produce a baby six months later.'

I can't help but smile at the thought, hoping I don't offend. Hettie seems to take none and continues her narrative.

At around this time, the pressure of work started to mount on Uncle. Although he and his team had completed much of their research, Uncle had not yet been able to factor in the human element in a way that the government would listen to him. The dean, wanting the accolade for the London School of Economics and Political Science, was pushing Uncle to give up on that aspect of his research and just publish the paper as it was. Uncle refused. He then upset the university's hierarchy with his outspoken comments on other aspects of the government's policy.

'England was sending shiploads of children to Australia,' Hettie says with outrage. 'Officially they were orphans, but a few stories were emerging where children left in temporary care, while their parents found jobs and tried to get back on their feet, had been sent off and were never to be seen or heard of again.'

This policy, one I had studied but I let Hettie give me her understanding of it, was solving an economic issue for England by shifting the cost of housing, feeding, and educating the children to the Australian Government. Plus, the children were the offspring of the lower classes, so it was much like the transportation of convicts; England was ridding its shores of the unwanted. What troubled Uncle was that no one was stopping to consider the impact this forced migration was having on the children.

Uncle was openly critical; the university didn't like this. They were worried about it negatively impacting their funding. It didn't matter anyway; the government wasn't listening. Whatever fallout occurred would happen years down the track and therefore the problem wouldn't be theirs.

'I guess it was the build-up of all those years of frustration, of Henry trying to do good and continually being knocked down. Henry was not supported by anyone in what he was trying to achieve. He'd seen so much pain and suffering, which he thought should have been avoided. It all became too much and a year after we were married, Henry had a nervous breakdown.

'One morning, he just couldn't face going to work. He couldn't face anyone,' Hettie says sadly. 'Henry withdrew from everyone and everything. He did nothing but sleep, eat, and walk the streets. Eventually, he stopped walking the streets too. He couldn't bear to see the poor people of London. He felt they were a constant reminder of his failure to do anything positive to help them.'

'A lot of people blamed me for the breakdown,' she says without rancour. 'Everyone thought he'd been alright until I came along. They didn't appreciate that this had been brewing for most of Henry's life. He'd set himself one goal, he just wanted to help people who were down and out, and he'd struggled for decades to achieve it with, he felt, no success. They didn't see his breakdown and withdrawal as a larger-scale repeat of his reaction to the uncomfortable things he had witnessed while travelling. They didn't see it as the result of years of witnessing the poor, the lower class, of England suffering.

'When he isolated himself, they thought that was my doing too. Of course, I inadvertently helped them think that. I thought Henry just needed some time out, so I'd negotiated a sabbatical with the university and we moved here to Charmouth, for what was supposed to be a year. But Henry never recovered enough to go back. He stayed here and stagnated for almost eleven years. And then you came along.'

෨෨෨෨෨෨

I am so surprised by everything Hettie has told me and so shocked at how clueless I've been, that for several minutes, I can only sit in stunned silence.

'I had no idea,' is all I can lamely offer.

'There's no reason why you should have known. I was never sure what your mother had said to you. I imagined nothing at first, but I thought maybe, when you were around thirteen or fourteen, she might have said something. You...well you changed a little to Henry around that time.'

'Yes I did change,' I acknowledge with much regret. 'But it was not to do with anything I'd been told. It was just me becoming a self-conscious teenager. Gosh, it all seems so petty when I look back on it now,' I say with angst and remorse. 'So childish on my part and yet I thought I was being mature. It's simply that I became a little embarrassed by Uncle's eccentricities. I'd heard Mother refer to Uncle as mad, and I worried a bit that, by association, I would also be considered mad. I didn't really have any friends my age and I wondered if that might be part of the reason why.

'I also wanted to step out of the constraints of my life, to live and to experience everything the world had to offer. It felt like Uncle was trying to keep me confined to his four walls, the barriers he seemed to have around him. I loved and admired Uncle so much, but I didn't want to be like him, I didn't want to live like he did.'

Hettie nods and I feel that she understands.

'Some of those eccentricities have always been there, they are just Henry, nothing to do with the breakdown. But yes, he did really confine and isolate himself after that. He didn't like to have to face what he was powerless to do anything about. He also became averse to change. Little things like moving where I kept the butter in the pantry could be enough to upset him. As you can see,' she says with a sweeping gesture of her hand. 'So as not to upset his equilibrium, I've made sure that nothing has changed around here in over thirty years.'

It occurs to me as Hettie tells me this, that she too has been a prisoner of Uncle's self-imposed confines and that she has, without complaint, restricted her life to accommodate Uncle's needs. I mention this to her now.

'I haven't minded,' she replies while not denying the truth of it. 'It was worse in the first seven or eight years that we lived here. Henry really did nothing except mope around the house. He didn't read, didn't go anywhere. But he did talk to me, so he has always remained good company. That's probably what stopped me from having a breakdown too.

'The first breakthrough I had in getting Henry to come out of himself a little, was when we adopted Floss. Henry took the responsibility of dog ownership very seriously. Having Floss meant that he had to take her out for a walk every day. When you consider that there had been periods, sometimes as long as several months, where I hadn't been able to get Henry to step over the threshold, that was quite something.'

'The walks made Henry realise that he enjoyed being outside, he felt better after his daily constitution with Floss. Then he developed an interest in gardening, so that was another outlet for him. Although he still wouldn't go into the township and he didn't really interact with other people unless forced to, at least he has an interest and a purpose to his life.'

My mind is still reeling and I have so much more that I want to understand, but I don't know where to begin. So, I start with me.

'Despite all of this, you still agreed to have me come to stay, I was a stranger after all. What would you have done if Uncle hadn't coped with me?'

'Thank goodness I never had to deal with that scenario, but yes I did initially worry about it. Henry didn't hesitate to say yes when your mother called, so I could only hope it would be alright. I must say that we were a bit surprised by the request, our communication with Helen was restricted to an exchange of Christmas cards only, and I know she was among the group of people who blamed me for Henry's breakdown. But we understood that she had no one else to turn to. And besides, having you come to stay for the summer was about you, not about her, so we agreed to her request.'

I can tell by Hettie's tone that this is all she wants to say about my mother. I'm happy to let the subject drop.

'Henry actually seemed quite excited at the prospect of having you here, and while I was a little concerned about his ability to cope, I thought we'd muddle through it all somehow and we did. I think, in retrospect, all Henry ever wanted was to be able to care for, and nurture, someone. As a young man, and until the breakdown, he lacked the confidence in his ability to do this on a one-to-one basis, that's why he attempted to do it for the whole world instead. Then you came along and you were such a lost and lonely little boy, very polite and so sweet, but so very much in need of love and nurturing.

'I think you and Henry helped each other grow. He became so alive and animated when you were here during the summers. I couldn't believe that first day when he kept you out all day. I was so worried about you both. Then you came home together and he looked like a new man, like his soul had returned to him. You inspired him to read again, to exercise his mind with research. Those encyclopaedias never gathered dust again like they had in our first decade here.

'He slumped back into his depression when you went home each year and that worried me. I was always concerned that he'd fall further into his pit of despair than he'd ever been before. I had to buoy him up with the weekly phone calls and the anticipation of you coming again next summer. And that worked, slowly each year his suffering at your departure was not as great. But you're right, you became an adult and left Henry behind a little.'

'Those phone calls were my lifeline, it never occurred to me they were Uncle's too!'

As though Uncle knows he is being talked about, he stirs in his sleep and slowly opens his eyes. He looks surprised and slightly alarmed, to see me sitting next to him on the lounge. He immediately looks to Hettie for reassurance.

'Joe and I have been catching up on news,' she tells him gently. The mention of my name re-orientates him.

'Did I fall asleep? Have I missed tea?'

'Goodness, look at the time,' responds Hettie with some alarm as she glances at the clock on the wall. 'I'd better get on with fixing something for you both to eat. Do you think you should go to the bathroom, Henry?'

'Probably,' says Uncle as he rises gingerly to his feet and heads off upstairs.

The environment and the routine he has here are so familiar and comforting that I wonder how he'll cope with the move to the nursing home. As Hettie rises to follow Uncle out of the door, I call out to her.

'Hettie, are you going to move into the nursing home too?'

Hettie stops in her tracks and comes back to perch on the lounge next to me. She puts a hand on my arms and then, as gently as she possibly can, she breaks my heart.

'No, Joe, I won't be. I'm so sorry to have to tell you this, but please don't say anything to Henry, he doesn't know. You see, I'm dying. I have ovarian cancer which has spread to my liver and to my bones. The doctor says I'll be lucky to live a few more weeks. I would never have let Henry be moved to a nursing home for any other reason than I won't be here to look after him.'

Chapter 15

I retreat to my bedroom as soon as I am able to and unashamedly cry like a baby. For Hettie to die is just unthinkable. As she herself said, she is twelve years younger than Uncle, the natural progression would be for her to at least see his life through.

I marvel at her calm acceptance of what is happening to her. But I guess what else can she do? Screaming and crying will not change anything. Maybe she ranted against her fate when she was first diagnosed, but I doubt it. Hettie seems to me to be the one who has always been calmly accepting of her lot, whatever that may be.

When I have finally shed every tear that I have in me, I go to the bathroom and wash my face, but as much as I try I cannot wash away the evidence of my crying. Then I go downstairs to join Uncle and Hettie for our evening meal. Hettie looks at me as I enter the room, and gives me a wan smile, but she says nothing. Uncle notices nothing unusual.

We all three act as though today is a day just like any other, which will be the same as tomorrow and every day thereafter. But Hettie and I both know it will and can never be the same again, while Uncle blissfully knows nothing.

After we've eaten, I usher Hettie and Uncle into the front room while I stay and do the dishes. When I join them, they are ready at the table with the pack of cards spread before them. Hettie suggests we play Snap, which surprises me at first until I wonder if this is because Uncle's powers of concentration aren't up to Gin Rummy. My thoughts are soon confirmed, for even Snap taxes Uncle's abilities. He misses some matches and tries to claim other matches that do not exist. I follow Hettie's lead and let Uncle do as he wants. He seems to be enjoying himself.

I wish that Clara were here, I so desperately want to tell her all that I've learnt. I feel a need to lighten the burden of my knowledge by sharing it with someone I love. I regret now that I never bought her here to stay for the night, that she will never really understand what my summers here with Uncle and Hettie were like.

Within an hour, Hettie looks washed out and tired and I suggest that she goes up to bed and I will sit with Uncle for a while. She has had sole responsibility for Uncle for so long that her mind fights against my suggestion. But her body is spent and she yields to my urgings. She makes me promise to wake her when Uncle comes up to bed, just so she can make sure that he settles off to sleep alright.

As I watch her leave the room, it occurs to me that the pinched look on her face and the stiffness in all of her movements have more to do with the pain from the cancer than with old age or tiredness as I'd originally thought. I wonder if she is suffering without medication, so many of the painkillers would have the side effect of making her sleepy, and with Uncle's unpredictable behaviour that is not something she can afford to be.

For all of my bravado in offering to look after Uncle and sending Hettie up to bed early, I am at first uncertain how to go about caring for him; it is a responsibility I have never had before. He sits on the couch and looks at me expectantly and I feel a sense of panic that there is something I must do to amuse him. In the end, I select a volume of the encyclopaedia from the bookshelf and Uncle and I spend an hour seated together on the lounge, reading about dinosaurs. Uncle chats away animatedly, recalling our days exploring for fossils on East Beach. When he looks like he is about to fall asleep where he sits, I suggest that it is time for bed. He quickly agrees and together we make our way upstairs.

Again, I follow Hettie's lead and simply suggest to him to use the bathroom and clean his teeth. Uncle follows all of my instructions like an obedient child. Our preparations for bed have woken Hettie long before we actually enter the bedroom. After seeing Uncle tucked in and getting assurances from Hettie that she'll manage from here on, I go to my room.

I undress and go through the motions of getting ready for sleep. My body is exhausted and my mind feels like it can't possibly think another thought, but sleep eludes me. I am stuck with the image of Uncle alone in a nursing home and Hettie nowhere in sight. After several hours of restlessly lying there, I get up and retrieve Percy from the chair under the window. With the comforting feel of his warm presence in my arms, I eventually drift off to sleep.

༆༆༆༆༆

The drizzle has stopped by the following morning, but the day is overcast with a cool breeze. I help Hettie in the kitchen with breakfast. She seems more and more willing to accept any assistance I have to offer. Uncle's appetite seems unabated, putting away a bowl of cereal and two slices of toast, while I can only pick half-heartedly at a single slice of toast. Hettie doesn't make any pretence of attempting to eat anything.

I talk to Hettie about pain medication and she admits that while the doctor has given her some, she has been reluctant to take any. I urge her to have some now and to lie down for a rest, I'll look after Uncle.

I get him well rugged up in his coat and scarf, for he needs my assistance, he no longer seems able to do these things for himself, and together we take Jess for a walk. We don't go very far. Uncle is limping slightly, an uncomfortable bruise on his hip, Hettie told me, and Jess has no energy for a long walk anymore. Uncle seems in good spirits, though. Apart from the bruise and a graze on his arm, he is showing no untoward effects from yesterday's escapade. There is no sign of a temperature and Hettie and I have both already agreed that a call to the doctor is not required.

When we return to the cottage, Jess goes immediately to the front porch and curls up in a ball. As I look at her lying there with flecks of grey showing through the black coat on her muzzle, I realise that I'll need to consider her future too. I quickly calculate that she must be over thirteen years old now, too old to resettle with anyone else, and she won't be able to stay here at the cottage without Uncle and Hettie. I haven't the energy to tackle that problem now so I put all thoughts of it firmly towards the back of my mind.

I wander around the garden with Uncle as he tells me what he's been planting. The chickens are long gone, and most of the garden is overrun with weeds. Some of the crops that he says he has planted are well out-of-season, but he doesn't seem to notice that nothing has come of them. I decide that the state of the garden doesn't matter, Uncle still enjoys pottering around out here and there seems no harm in letting him do so.

I make lunch for Uncle and myself. Despite my urgings, Hettie can't bring herself to eat anything. This worries me greatly and I wonder how long she can go on for if she will take nothing to eat. I resolve to call the office first thing in the morning and request as much leave as I possibly can. I will not leave Hettie to die here alone. Nor will I see Uncle taken to a nursing home any sooner than he has to be.

However, despite this resolve, arrangements still have to be made and so after lunch, I head off to look at one of the nursing homes Hettie has on her list. I decide to stop at the café on the way and buy some chocolate éclairs for Uncle's afternoon tea.

There are three nursing homes in the nearby vicinity that Hettie believes might be worth looking at, although one she has already largely discounted because it is too far away from Charmouth.

'I think Henry will be more comfortable if he at least has a view of a familiar landscape,' she tells me.

I'm not certain it will help, but decide to focus my attention on the two closer facilities to begin with. The nearest one is just outside of the township; a large home which can accommodate over sixty residents. From the moment I drive up the driveway, I hate it. I realise that I am probably not in the best frame of mind for this task, but I wonder if any frame of mind would ever help me look favourably at this institution.

The home is a beautiful old building, possibly once a private residence for some lord of the region. It is set on several acres of land, and the grounds are beautiful, well-maintained and no doubt full of radiant colour at various times throughout the seasons. A few hardy residents are strolling on the pathways as I drive up and park the car. I imagine the rest of them have opted to remain indoors on an inclement day like today.

Being a Sunday, the matron is on her day off, but a stout, no-nonsense, senior sister offers to show me around. She explains that there is a mixture of shared and private rooms, with several communal bathrooms. The bathrooms are all modern and have the latest fittings to assist in the comfortable care of the elderly. Throughout our tour, she continually refers to them as "the elderly" and this annoys me. It's like they are a separate, sub-set, an "almost-species" of humans.

The main lounge and dining areas are on the ground floor, but there are a few sitting nooks with well-padded armchairs scattered across the first floor. The building is light and airy and tastefully decorated. The residents all seem comfortable and well cared for. Some are seated around tables playing cards or other board games, while others sit in armchairs quietly reading. A few sit staring vacantly into nothing.

A notice board in the main lounge tells me this is individual free time and that a sing-along will commence in half an hour, followed by visiting time. The timetable for this morning was filled with a variety of church services for the many different denominations of faith.

I'm introduced to several staff members, all of whom seem pleasant enough, if somewhat harried and distant. They are all dressed in the same uniform reinforcing the impression that this is nothing more than a nicely decorated institution, with no space for free thinking or individuality.

The sister asks me a number of questions about Uncle; his age, physical abilities, medical history, and continence status. Finally, she asks if he is prone to wandering and I am uncertain how to answer this question. She sees my hesitation.

'We don't have residents who wander,' she tells me firmly. 'Our other residents, particularly the ladies, don't like to have men in the home who may enter inappropriately into their rooms. Besides, those who wander take up too many nursing resources just for one person.'

I can't fault anything about the home, except for the fact that everything about it screams institutional and impersonal and that is not where I want Uncle to be. I thank the sister and leave.

Back at the cottage, Uncle is thrilled by the prospect of chocolate éclairs for afternoon tea. Without thinking, I asked for three when I bought them. Hettie shakes her head when I offer her one. I give it to Uncle instead.

While Uncle is distracted with this treat, Hettie asks me quietly about my impression of the home. 'It looked quite nice in the brochures,' she tells me.

I assure her that it was very nice and that it definitely is a potential option to be considered, but I don't want to make any decisions until I have looked at the other place. Hettie seems satisfied with that.

We pass the evening with reading and cards. With very little urging, Hettie retires early again and I stay up with Uncle. Hettie wakes up with a slight groan when I escort Uncle into the bedroom. Whether it is from the pain in her body or distress at being disturbed I don't know, but she assures me with a sleepy, slurred voice that she will take over Uncle's care from here.

'Joe. Joe, are you awake?'

Uncle's voice startles me from a deep sleep and for a moment I am disorientated; his summons taking me back to my childhood. But I soon realise, from the cramped conditions of the single bed that I am lying in, that I am here, in his cottage, as an adult now. As the recollection of the knowledge I have gained in the last few days comes flooding back to me, I wish fervently that I could still be a child and that Uncle is here simply to rouse me to go out on an adventure, but I know deep down that something is wrong.

'What's the problem, Uncle?'

I have no idea what the time is, but I can see through the partly closed curtain that it is still dark outside.

'Hettie won't wake up for a cup of tea.'

For a moment, my world goes black and I struggle for breath. Don't panic, I tell myself, Don't panic. But I quickly rise from my bed and push past Uncle onto the landing towards their bedroom. He moves to follow me but I stop him.

'Why don't you go downstairs and put the kettle on again, I wouldn't mind a cup of tea myself. I'll see to Hettie.'

'Okay, Joe.'

Uncle totters down the stairs, happy with his task and relieved of his worry. I turn back to the bedroom door but hesitate to step over the threshold. Taking a deep breath and stiffening my resolve, I reach inside the door frame and flick on the light switch.

The blankets on Uncle's side of the bed, furthest away from the door, lie in an untidy tangle. He has pulled them down slightly as he slipped out of bed and in doing so has exposed Hettie's shoulder and upper arm to the cold. Hettie is facing away from me, lying quite still on her side as though watching over the slight indentation in the mattress that once nestled Uncle's body. The room is deathly quiet.

With my heart in the pit of my stomach, I slowly walk around the foot of the bed so that I can look into Hettie's face. Her grey hair has been released from the confines of her habitual bun and lies spread across the pillow, she obviously didn't have the energy to plait it as she would usually have done. The pinched, somewhat anxious, look has gone from her face. I would not call her expression peaceful, merely just restful. The grey pallor is gone and her skin has assumed a sharp white colour with a blue undertone, as though it is covered with a layer of frost.

I reach out to touch her hand, to feel for a pulse, but there is nothing. I let my hand gently caress against her face. Her skin is dry and textured and feels very cold. I remember how silky-smooth and warm it once was and how I had snuggled against it for comfort on my first night in this house. Gently, I reach down and place a kiss on her cold cheek.

'Joe.'

Uncle's voice, slightly high-pitched with anxiety, wafts over to me from where he stands in the doorway.

'Yes, Uncle.'

'Hettie's not well, is she?'

I struggle to find the right answer to the question. How do I explain to him what has happened?

'No,' I finally manage to say. 'I'm going to go downstairs and call the doctor.'

'Okay. I'll sit with Hettie while you're gone.'

I leave him lying on the bed beside her. He has taken Hettie's hand from where it rested on the pillow and placed it on his cheek as though he wished for her to caress him.

By the clock on the wall in the front room, I discover that it is only five in the morning. I debate for a moment if it is too early to call the doctor, but determine that I have no other option. It is not until after he has answered the phone, his voice heavy with sleep, that I realise this is a pointless exercise. Hettie is dead, there is nothing the doctor can do, I could have let him sleep on. I'm sure he realises this too, but he reassuringly tells me that he'll be there as soon as he can.

Unwilling to disturb Uncle's time with Hettie, I wander into the kitchen to wait. The mug of tea that Uncle was making for me sits on the table, next to one the one he made earlier for Hettie. I pick it up to take a sip but am unable to bring myself to drink it; it seems wrong to take in sustenance while Hettie lies cold upstairs.

The doctor arrives within twenty minutes. He has slipped into a pair of jeans and just thrown a jumper on over his pyjama top. He is younger than I expected, possibly late thirties, and this surprises me. I had just assumed that Hettie would feel more comfortable with someone older, especially given the location of her cancer. Such a silly assumption, I tell myself. We introduce ourselves and I explain what has happened.

'Uncle is still upstairs with Hettie, would you prefer that I ask him to come down?'

'No, I think it might be better for Henry if we all do this together.'

I understand from this that he is familiar with Uncle and is under no illusion as to how difficult this will be for him.

I nod my agreement and we make our way up the stairs. Uncle is still lying on the bed beside Hettie. There are tears rolling down his face and it occurs to me for the first time this morning that although Uncle has dementia, this does not mean he is going to be ignorant of what is happening.

'Hello, Henry. It's Doctor Gregg. Do you remember me?'

'Yes, but Hettie's not very well, can you make her better?'

Uncle's apprehension, and his childlike desire for a cure where there can be no cure is touching; I feel the tears well in my eyes. I notice a glistening of moisture in the doctor's eyes as well, and I like him all the better for that.

'Let me just have a listen to her heart, and we'll see.'

The doctor removes his stethoscope from his bag and Uncle and I watch anxiously as he listens for Hettie's heartbeat. Uncle's optimism is infectious, and stupidly I feel a faint stirring of hope; maybe Hettie is not dead, just deeply asleep and the doctor can do something to make her better. It is a forlorn hope.

The doctor removes the stethoscope buds from his ears, and reaches out to put a hand on Uncle's shoulder.

'I'm sorry, Henry,' he says gently. 'But Hettie has left us.'

Uncle doesn't rail or rant, he just buries his head in his pillow and cries uncontrollably. Tears well in my eyes and a large lump forms in my throat. I have to struggle to keep my composure. The doctor motions to me and together we step out onto the landing where he offers me his condolences.

'Hettie was a beautiful, selfless lady,' he tells me and I can only nod in agreement, if I spoke I feel I would lose control. He suggests that I sit with Uncle while he calls the undertaker.

'It will be hard for Henry,' he adds as he turns to walk down the stairs. 'He understands now what has happened, but with his short-term memory loss there is every possibility that he will forget later and then have to go through the trauma of re-learning about Hettie's passing.'

I nod as though I understand what he is saying, but I am not sure I understand much of what is happening at the moment. The doctor continues downstairs and I return to the bedroom.

I am not sure how to approach Uncle, *how do you comfort someone when their life partner has just died?* The best I can think to do is to sit beside him on the bed and rub his back and shoulder. He does not rebuff my touch. Eventually, his sobs subside a little, but he neither moves nor speaks.

When I hear the sound of the undertaker's car pulling up outside, I suggest to Uncle that it is time for us to go downstairs. He is silently compliant. I assist him in putting on a dressing gown, realising belatedly that he must be cold, dressed only in his pyjamas with no bedclothes covering him. I curse myself for not having thought of this sooner, I am obviously not used to having to think for someone else.

At the doorway, I turn and wish Hettie a final goodbye. Then I lead Uncle downstairs and into the kitchen, leaving Doctor Gregg to manage the removal of Hettie's body. I put the kettle on and make some tea, which Uncle and I sip half-heartedly until the doctor joins us.

He provides me with the Undertaker's details and advises that I should get in touch with them later today or tomorrow to discuss the arrangements. I ask if there is anything special I need to do for Uncle, but he tells me that just being with him will be enough for now. He does leave me some tablets; sedation for Uncle if he seems too distressed. He promises to look in on us tomorrow and then he is gone.

I look at the clock; it is only just past seven in the morning and already so much has happened in our day.

ശശശശശ

It is hard to stay focused and think clearly, so I take the rest of the day one step at a time. Uncle and I shower and dress. I am grateful that Uncle is still capable of attending to his daily hygiene for himself, he only needs prompting on what to do and he can take it from there. I do worry about what he might be doing the whole time I am in the shower, but in the end, I needn't have hurried. He is still sitting on the lounge where I left him, staring vacantly into space.

Going into his bedroom, I strip and wash the sheets, making up the bed with fresh linen. We take Jess for a walk. I go through the motions of making breakfast and lunch, but neither of us eats much. I also call my office and arrange to take two weeks' leave, effective immediately.

From Uncle, I am able to find out the names of Hettie's brother and sister. In the address book, I find their contact details, neatly written in Hettie's sloping handwriting. They have both immigrated, one to Australia and one to Canada. Without stopping to think of the time difference, I call them both. They are surprised by the news and saddened, but distant in their responses. They don't ask after Uncle and I get the impression that although family, Hettie's communication with her siblings had become an exchange of Christmas cards only. They will not be coming for the funeral.

I ask Uncle if I should notify anyone else, but he is vague in his answer. Knowing that he and Hettie have been an insular unit of only two people for the last thirty years, even within their local community, I do not pursue the topic. I do, however, place a notice in the London papers. Surely those who worked with Hettie at the university would like to know.

I long to call Clara. Because she has been out of phone contact for the weekend I have not even been able to tell her the news that Hettie is ill, let alone the events of today. She will not be home until this evening, so I reluctantly acknowledge that I will have to wait until then.

Uncle has a nap on the couch after lunch and wakes up still knowing what has happened. This is distressing, but also a relief at the same time. I try to ask him about the funeral arrangements, but he tells me that he and Hettie never discussed it so I should do what I think is best. I contact the undertakers and arrange for a cremation at two in the afternoon on Wednesday, there seems no point in delaying it any longer.

I offer to read Uncle a chapter from *"Watership Down"*, but he says that wouldn't be right, reading aloud was something only Hettie used to do. I understand how he feels, most of the tasks I have undertaken today are things that I've never done here before, inside of the house was always Hettie's domain. In fact, I determine, as I think the matter over, in over twenty years of visits I have never once been in the house without Hettie being present. The thought of this chills me.

Finally, early in the evening, I manage to get hold of Clara. She has just walked in the door and is tired, but happy from her weekend away. I cry as I tell her the news. I'm not sure I really made much sense, but she seemed to understand the brevity of the situation and my level of distress. It is too late for her to come to Charmouth now, and she has a few things she needs to sort out for work tomorrow, but she tells me she hopes to be here by tomorrow evening. I relay this news to Uncle and he responds by asking who Clara is.

When it becomes time for bed, I worry about how Uncle will cope. *How will it be for him to climb into a bed he shared with Hettie for so many years and not have her there beside him?* He doesn't mention it as an issue and I certainly don't raise it. He has been mostly silent all day and has not cried again since this morning. At the moment, he looks exhausted, quite shattered by the day's events. I wait outside the bedroom door until I hear the sound of him snoring before I go to my own bed, but I can't settle.

To farewell Hettie was not the reason I came here. The true purpose of my visit, settling Uncle into a nursing home, was always going to be hard and emotionally draining, but Hettie's death has totally flattened me. So many thoughts and memories come flooding through my brain. Some of them are good and make me smile, like the image of Hettie tapping her foot on the floor, with her hands on her hip and calling Uncle "incorrigible". Or the one of her refusing to give Uncle his slice of custard tart until he'd promised to always make sure I'd had breakfast every morning before we went out exploring. Certainly, the vision of Hettie swamped in pale golden light handing me Percy on my first night here brings both smiles and tears. Other images, more recent ones such as her wan figure and hunched posture, just make me cry.

Behind all of these thoughts sits my fear and apprehension about what is to become of Uncle. Not the least of my worries is how impossible it is for me to sleep in case he decides to wander out, naked, into the night.

Chapter 16

I awake with a start. The cottage is in darkness and everything is quiet; too quiet. I rise quickly to my feet and cross the landing to Uncle's bedroom. Although the curtains are tightly closed, letting in no chink of light, I am able to see enough to know that there is no discernible figure lying in the bed. To be sure, I flick on the light switch.

Just like yesterday morning, Uncle has left the blankets in a tangled mess in the middle of the bed. On top of this, lies his pyjama top. There is no sign of Uncle. I hurry downstairs. The front door is closed and locked, just as I left it. I check the front room and then the kitchen. Here I feel a draught and realise that the back door is wide open. I step onto the back porch, where I can clearly see Uncle; the whiteness of his naked chest is glistening in the hint of moonlight. He is walking around the garden, stopping to look under shrubs and pick up pots to see what might lie underneath. He is mumbling to himself, but his voice is too indistinct for me to make out what he is saying. I call out his name and he snaps his head upright and peers in my direction.

'Hettie is that you? Where have you been hiding?'

'No, Uncle. It's me, Joe. What are you doing out there?'

'I'm looking for Hettie. I can't find her anywhere.'

I feel a pain in my heart, Dr Gregg's prediction is coming true. Wearily, I call out to Uncle to come back inside. He does so obediently, which is a relief. His feet are wet and the moisture from the damp ground has seeped up the trouser legs of his pyjamas. His skin feels icy to touch, but he is not shivering.

I usher him upstairs to the shower and keep him busy with the acts of bathing and dressing. I don't want to have the conversation about Hettie any earlier than I have to. While Uncle is in the shower, I go back downstairs to make him a cup of tea. When I glance at the clock, I am shocked to discover that it is only half-past two in the morning. I change tactics and put some milk on the stove, hoping that a mug of cocoa might help Uncle to settle back to sleep. When I go back upstairs, he is standing at the door to his bedroom, thankfully dressed in the clean pyjamas that I put out for him.

'Hettie's still not here,' he says to me forlornly looking at the crumpled mess that is his bed.

'I've made you some cocoa to help you settle for the night. It's way too early to be up and about,' I respond with forced cheerfulness.

'But what about Hettie?'

Obviously, I can defer this conversation no longer. Gently, with my arm around his shoulders, I remind Uncle of what happened just yesterday. Uncle gives a loud sigh but does not break down in tears. Refusing the cocoa, he clambers back into bed, facing away from where I stand in the doorway.

'Are you okay, Uncle? Can I get you anything?'

Uncle does not respond. I flick off the light switch and go into my room, leaving both bedroom doors wide open. I move my chair from under the window and place it in the middle of the room where I can look over at Uncle. He doesn't stir but I can tell from his breathing that he is not asleep. I drink the cocoa, but I don't sleep either.

༺༺༺༺༺༺

In the morning, Uncle is very subdued. He looks grey and haggard and slightly shrunken like the life has been sucked out of him. We go through the pretence of eating breakfast and then we take Jess for a walk. Uncle seems well enough, but I worry about the effects of his two recent exposures to the outside elements.

Doctor Gregg calls in as promised and gives Uncle a quick examination. Uncle does not object, merely co-operates passively. After he has finished, I ask the doctor to step into the kitchen while I leave Uncle resting in the front room. Uncle has no interest in doing anything; he just sits on the couch staring into nothing.

The doctor reassures me that physically Uncle is fine, but there are only so many times a man of his age can go outside naked in winter without doing himself harm. I question what the nakedness is about, what does it signify? Doctor Gregg can't say for sure, but he thinks it is just a case of mixed messages in Uncle's brain.

'Henry knows that when he gets out of bed he has to do something about clothes, but he can't remember what. His options are to put something on, like his dressing gown, or take something off. Sometimes he gets it right, but that is pure luck, and sometimes he gets it wrong.'

We discuss nursing homes but I demure about making any decisions. There is one home left to be seen, so I can't decide yet. However, my main concern is more about the distress to Uncle. His life has imploded already; he has lost Hettie I don't want him to lose his familiar surroundings as well.

'I'm here for two more weeks,' I tell the doctor. 'I can care for Uncle in the meantime.'

'Have you ever cared for an elderly person with dementia before?' he asks me kindly, but firmly. I have to admit not, but how hard can it be?

'I'll manage,' is the only response I feel able to give.

Doctor Gregg nods understandingly but warns me not to wear myself out. 'You don't look like you got much sleep last night.'

I can't argue with that, but at the moment my sleep doesn't seem important. As the doctor takes his leave, he reminds me that I have some sedatives for Uncle.

'Use them if need be,' he advises. 'For both of your sakes.'

After lunch, it is necessary to go to Charmouth for some supplies and also to visit the funeral parlour to finalise the arrangements for Hettie's funeral tomorrow. What am I to do with Uncle? I obviously can't leave him here, so he has no choice but to come with me. Surprisingly, he doesn't object. I am stunned. In all of my summers here, Uncle always refused to come into Charmouth with Hettie and I. He travelled only as far as his legs could carry him and only went in directions that were full of nature and very few people. Maybe the idea of being alone in the house is more frightening for him than coming with me.

In Charmouth, I ask if he wants to come into the shop with me, but he says no, he'll stay in the car. This worries me, can I trust him not to wander off? I try to tempt him to come with me by offering him the opportunity to come into the café and select his treat for afternoon tea, but he won't budge. In the end, I leave him in the car and dash quickly into the shop to grab some bread and milk and a can of baked beans. When I come out, Uncle is still in the car, so I make another quick dash into the café to purchase a custard tart for afternoon tea.

Altogether, this takes me no longer than five minutes and Uncle is still waiting passively in the car when I get back. That was lucky, but I can't help but wonder if I will always be so fortunate on future outings. At the funeral parlour, Uncle does agree to come in with me. They are expecting us, for I rang to make an appointment, but even so, we have to spend a few minutes waiting in the reception room. There is a sombre darkness to the building, despite the cream-coloured walls and mass of brightly coloured flowers in the large vase on the table in the middle of the room.

Uncle seems unnerved by the surroundings and sticks close to me; he is like a child who is scared that they might get separated from their parent in a crowd. The undertaker approaches us with a quiet dignified air. I wonder if this is his natural bearing, or whether it has taken years of practice. I would rather he smiled; his degree of solemness over the death of someone he did not know is uncomfortable for me.

We are led into a small interview room where I have to make decisions about the flowers, coffins, music and the service. Uncle contributes nothing to these plans, just looks warily around him. I try to ask him questions, what music would Hettie have liked, and what was her favourite flower, but he doesn't answer. His only response is when I ask him if he wants to say something at the service.

'No, Joe. I wouldn't know what to say. Would you mind doing it?'

We are offered the option of refreshments after the service. I don't expect any other mourners apart from ourselves, so I decline the offer.

This done, Uncle and I return home to find Clara waiting.

೪೪೪೪೪

It is such a relief to see Clara that I break down in tears as I hug her. She hugs me back tightly and runs her fingers gently through my hair. I don't know how long I bury my head on her shoulder, but after what seems like ages I feel Uncle's hand giving me a comforting pat on the back.

'It's okay, Joe,' I hear him murmur. 'Don't cry now.'

When we'd first arrived home and seen Clara sitting on the front porch patting Jess, who sat adoringly beside her, Uncle had been slightly perturbed.

'Who is that woman?' he'd demanded to know as I pulled my car to the side of the road. 'Why is she patting Floss like that?'

'It's Jess, not Floss, Uncle. We haven't had Floss for such a long time now. Remember.'

'I know it's Jess. But who's that woman?'

'That's Clara, my wife. You've met Clara, she's been here to visit before,' I'd replied wearily.

'Yes, I know that, but why is she here now?'

'She's here to help look after us. We need looking after because we're a bit lost without Hettie.'

'She's not replacing Hettie!'

Uncle was indignant, something I'd never known him to be. Unable to deal with him at that moment, I'd simply ended the conversation by getting out of the car and going to hug Clara. The sight of my distress, the first time I'd shown it to Uncle, obviously diffused his mood and he too attempted to join Clara in comforting me.

My tears dried, we all go inside and I leave Clara and Uncle in the kitchen while I go to wash my face. When I return, I find them working reasonably companionable together, putting away the supplies that I'd bought. Clara, sensitive to how Uncle might feel about a stranger interfering in Hettie's domain, is asking where she should put the loaf of bread. Uncle, either because he's forgotten or he's never known, is saying that it doesn't matter she can put it anywhere in the pantry. I point out the bread bin to Clara, an intrusion on Hettie's domain that Uncle doesn't seem to mind.

I make the tea and we seat ourselves around the table; Uncle and I in our usual places and Clara in the seat that has mostly been vacant. I almost regret that no one sits in Hettie's seat; its emptiness screams of our loss.

Uncle is tempted by the custard tart and while he eats and drinks his first real piece of sustenance since Sunday night, Clara and I talk about little things like the traffic on the roads and the weather in London. Having sat quietly in his own world and eaten his tart and drank two cups of tea, Uncle suddenly perks up and participates lucidly in the conversation.

'You're a vet, aren't you, Clara?'

Both of us are surprised by this question, after never seeming to be able to remember Clara's name, or who she is, Uncle can suddenly recall her occupation.

'Yes, Henry. I work in a small clinic in Twickenham. Mostly I look after cats and dogs, but I get the occasional bird or hamster too. I even had to look after a miniature pig the other day.'

'That must be a nice job. Animals are so lovely.'

'Well, not always that lovely,' responds Clara with a laugh. 'I've got a few scars I could show you from where a couple of dogs have not appreciated my ministrations.'

'I've only ever had dogs as pets, not cats. That's Jess you were patting. She's our second dog, before that we had Floss. Do you think that Jess has got arthritis? She seems so very stiff in the back legs some mornings.'

'I'm quite sure she has arthritis, but that's not surprising at her age. Does she have any medication for it?'

'No. The vet here has never given us any.'

'I can give you something for her if you like. It will ease the pain in her joints a little and remove some of that stiffness.'

Uncle thanks Clara and then his moment of lucidity ceases as he asks me if it is time for bed yet. I tell him no and suggest that if he's tired, he might like to have a rest on the couch. Without another word, he wanders over to the front room and lies down. He does not close his eyes, just stares vacantly at the ceiling.

Clara and I are now able to talk frankly. I tell her all that has happened, leaving nothing out regarding Uncle's escapades.

'I don't understand the disease,' I tell her. 'Sometimes, like just then with you, he seems so tuned in to what is going on and at other times he is off with the fairies. I just never know which Uncle I'm going to be faced with.'

Clara asks about nursing homes and again I demure from any sort of definite answer. I'm just not ready to deal with that issue yet. Clara doesn't push the point but I can tell she thinks I have no other option than to seek placement for him so I might as well get on with it.

We pass the evening in the front room. Clara and I read quietly while Uncle stares at nothing. He refuses offers to play cards or to continue with "*Watership Down*". When we come to retire, I realise that haven't thought things through very well. There is only a single bed in my room and there is no way Clara and I will manage any sleep if we attempt to lie there together. In the end, I give Clara the bed while I opt to sleep on the couch. Down here, I hope I can be alert to any attempts on Uncle's part to leave the house, naked or otherwise. In the end, I didn't need to have worried. Tired from a lack of sleep over the previous few days, Uncle sleeps like a baby until eight the following morning.

ೞೞೞೞೞ

Doctor Gregg is at Hettie's funeral, for which I am very grateful; it is a kind thing for him to do. I had worried that it would feel odd to deliver a eulogy to such a small audience, but I discover it's not about who's there to hear, it's just about remembering Hettie. I'd made a few notes, but mainly I talk from the heart; just letting my memories of Hettie ramble through my head and out of my mouth.

Uncle sits quietly; a single tear running down his cheek. He gives a tiny smile when I focus on a memory that is particularly poignant for him, but otherwise, he shows no emotion. Within thirty minutes, it is all over and Hettie's coffin is taken to the crematorium.

I invite Doctor Gregg home for a cup of tea, but he is off to an appointment with a client. He tells me to call him any time if I need to.

Uncle, Clara, and I go home where none of us feel like doing anything, not even having scones for afternoon tea.

Chapter 17

The evening is spent listlessly. I find it is hard to settle when I am surrounded by every physical, tangible reminder of someone who is lost to me in all but thought. Uncle doesn't speak, except when spoken to directly; he just sits in his spot on the couch and stares at nothing. Clara attempts to make something for us to eat, but Uncle refuses all food and drink. I make an effort to pick at the omelette she has cooked, but only because I don't want to hurt Clara's feelings.

The night that follows is dreadful. Uncle is up twice, confused and disorientated both times. The first time Clara hears him in the bathroom and comes downstairs to get me. I find him fully dressed for the day time, and trying to shave his whiskers. He has cut himself badly, just under his chin and this is bleeding freely. The blood trickles down his throat and stains the collar of his shirt. It takes quite some time to get the bleeding to stop, and I am no first-aider. In the end, I resort to using the pressure from several firmly applied sticking plasters to staunch the flow of blood.

Uncle insists that it is time to take Jess for a walk and at first refuses to believe that it is still the middle of the night. Even when I make him look out of the window into the dark, he will not believe me. I don't really know how to handle this situation, am I making things worse or helping him to understand where he is? Finally, my persistence wins through and he consents to get back into his pyjamas and go back to bed.

Clara, confident that I am in charge of the situation, has firmly closed the bedroom door and returned to her bed. I understand this isn't her problem. I make sure that Uncle is comfortably settled again before I return to lie wakefully on the couch. It is only a quarter to one.

I let my brain ponder the issue of Uncle, and what to do with him. Practically, I tell myself, I have no option but to seek placement in a nursing home, but my whole being feels revolted by the idea. I have just drifted off to sleep again when banging noises in the kitchen wake me. I hasten off the couch in case Uncle is about to escape out of the backdoor. He is not. He is fossicking through the pantry, looking for an egg he tells me. He has a gas burner on with an empty saucepan on top; this is already starting to tarnish from the heat.

'Uncle! What are you doing?'

I admit I am exasperated and that my tone is sharp, but it is only two-thirty in the morning and I feel like I haven't slept for days.

'I fancy a boiled egg and some soldiers,' Uncle responds, not heeding my tone. 'Would you like some too?'

Pleased that he is finally having something to eat, but not pleased about the timing and the danger he is causing, I offer to boil the egg for him. I cut a slice of bread to toast and put the kettle on to boil. Uncle sits and we both sip our tea. Obviously thirsty from his earlier fasting, Uncle drinks two large mugs full. This worries me slightly because I can see that yet a third awakening during the night will be required for a visit to the toilet. But it can't be helped. After he has finished, I usher Uncle back upstairs.

'What about Jess?' he asks, reluctant to go back to bed. 'I always walk Jess after breakfast. When will we walk her if we don't walk her now?'

'In the morning, Uncle. I'll come and wake you when it's morning and we'll go then okay?'

Uncle agrees and allows me to lead him back upstairs to his bedroom.

'It used to be me who would wake you in the mornings,' he says softly as we reached the top of the landing. I can only nod my head with fond remembrance.

I am reluctant to leave Uncle until I am sure he is asleep so I sit myself down on the little stool by Hettie's dressing table and wait. A long time passes and I can tell by Uncle's breathing that he is still awake. Silently, I wait some more.

'Joe.'

'Yes, Uncle.'

'Why did Hettie die?'

'Hettie had cancer, Uncle, ovarian cancer.'

I don't hesitate to speak the truth. I feel there is nothing to be gained from evasion or lying. Hettie has died and there is nothing more to shelter Uncle from. He seems to understand and accepts my answer, for he asks nothing further. But he does not go to sleep.

'Joe.'

'Yes, Uncle.'

'Did Hettie tell me she had cancer?'

'No Uncle. She didn't know herself until a few weeks ago. She didn't tell you then because she didn't want to worry you, there was nothing that you, or anyone else, could do.'

'That's good. I'd hate to think that she'd told me and that I'd forgotten. It would be a terrible thing to forget something like that.'

This information and reassurance seems to comfort Uncle, for he rolls over onto his side and nestles himself as though in preparation for sleep. I can only hope that my approach in telling the truth has been the right thing to do. Never before have I had to question so many of my actions in such a short time. Maybe it is possible that I do know how to care for Uncle.

A short time later, Uncle's light snores tell me that he has fallen back to sleep. I sit with him for a little while longer and then I return to my couch, but I am unable to sleep.

ഇഇഇഇഇ

The first rooster starts crowing long before dawn. I lie there listening to the sounds of the country and realise it is a long time since I've heard anything other than traffic noise. As a child, here in Charmouth, Uncle taught me to be still and just listen to the little sounds around me. There were so many sounds I was simply unaware of: bird songs, buzzing bees, and chirping insects, you could miss them all unless you stopped to listen. I tried stopping to listen in London, but there I only heard traffic rumbling and people shouting. They were not sounds I liked so I stopped listening then.

When dawn finally starts to lighten the sky, I get up. I clean up the mess in the kitchen and set about organising some breakfast for Clara and Uncle.

'You look like crap,' Clara says by way of a greeting some minutes later.

'It wasn't my best night's sleep ever!'

Coming to stand beside me, Clara puts her arm around my waist and leans her head against my shoulder. I return the embrace.

'Joe, this can't go on. You have to find somewhere for Henry to live. Or maybe someone to come here and look after him in his own home if you don't like the idea of a nursing home. But either way, you have to do something.'

'I know, Clara. I know,' I respond moving from her embrace and turning to gather bowls and spoons for breakfast. 'But it's not that easy. Uncle and Hettie took me in when I was alone and vulnerable. Uncle is alone and vulnerable now and it seems wrong to abandon him at this time.'

'Joe.' Clara turns me around to face her again and cups her hands on either side of my face so that I am forced to look directly into her eyes. 'Finding somewhere safe and secure for Henry to live is not abandoning him. It's doing the right thing, the best thing, for him.'

I am forced to acknowledge the truth of this and I tell her so, but I have the two weeks off from work already arranged, so I might as well use them to stay and care for Uncle. I also say that I have resolved to visit the other nursing home today.

'What about Jess, though?' I ask. 'What will I do with her?'

Clara smiles and then kisses me.

'Jess can come and live with us. They won't mind at the surgery if she comes with me to work every day. We lost Blackie, the cat, last week so we need a replacement surgery pet. Do you want me to take her with me today?'

'You're going today?'

'Yes, I have to. I did tell you that I could only get yesterday off from work. I have to do the afternoon shift today and then I'm on over the weekend.'

'Oh right. I'm sorry I forgot. My mind is too full of…'

'It's okay, Joe,' Clara interrupts me. 'I understand. And I understand that you have to stay and deal with things here your way. Just don't let it drain everything out of you.'

I hug Clara tightly, grateful for her love, patience and understanding. We agree to leave Jess for the moment. I can bring her with me when I return to London after Uncle is settled. I go upstairs to shower and dress before going in to wake Uncle. He is already awake, just lying quietly on his side of the bed with one arm thrown over the vacant part of the bed where Hettie used to lie.

'Ready to walk, Jess?'

Uncle nods and rises I hover on the landing as he showers and dresses in case he needs help, but he seems to manage by himself. I remove the wad of sticking plasters from his chin and am pleased to see the wound does not bleed again. We join Clara in the kitchen for breakfast.

After I have cleaned up and washed the dishes, I phone the other nursing home and make arrangements to visit this afternoon. Clara is now packed and ready to go. Uncle thanks her for helping Jess's arthritis, he thinks she seems less stiff this morning. I'm pleased, although surprised, that he remembers that whole conversation.

Clara gives him a hug and says she hopes to see him again soon. Uncle just nods and goes to call Jess. I hug Clara tightly and promise to call tonight after she has finished evening surgery. Reluctantly, we part. Clara gets into the car and drives away. I turn back to Uncle.

'Nice girl, that,' he tells me.

'Yes,' I agree. 'She is.'

Together, we head off down the laneway with Jess trotting at our heels. Uncle is right, she does seem to have lost some of her stiffness. We manage to walk further than we have on any other day and in the end it is the weather that turns us back towards home. I don't remember the sun shining since I arrived, and today is no exception. The clouds hang low and it's not long before the misty rain is falling softly around us.

Over a cup of tea in the cottage kitchen, it occurs to me that with Clara gone I have no choice but to take Uncle with me to view the nursing home. I ponder for a long time what to say about the purpose of our visit. In the end, I decide to say nothing. I don't want to cause unnecessary upset and it seems pointless to talk about the possibility of Uncle going to live there until it actually is a possibility.

ଔଔଔଔଔ

This nursing home is more centrally located in the town of Charmouth. I have driven past it countless times with Hettie on our weekly trips into the township without ever realising what it was. Essentially, it looks like any other house, only much larger than your average family home. The garden is a typical cottage garden; a little overgrown and untidy. In the backyard, I later discover, there are several vegetable plots much like those at Uncle's cottage. Residents, who have an interest, are encouraged to tend the gardens. There are several stone and wooden bench seats dotted throughout both the vegetable and the flower gardens. They are designed to give a few moments of respite to the active, unlike the chairs at the other home, which seemed designed to make the residents as inactive and quiet as possible.

I knock on the front door, which is opened by a young woman who is casually dressed in jeans and a t-shirt. She doesn't look like a staff member and at first; I mistake her for a visitor. She introduces herself as Michelle, one of the carers, and invites us into a comfortable front room while she goes to fetch Moira.

Moira, it turns out, would have been called matron at the other home, but here they prefer first names only.

'There is no such formality in a family home,' Moira explains. 'So why introduce it in this home?'

Moira offers to show Uncle around the house and he accepts with just a nod of his head. I tag along. There are only twelve residents in the house. All rooms are private, with private bathroom facilities. The philosophy of the home is to keep the residents as active as possible, so although all meals are provided and cleaners are employed, those who live in the house can do as much or as little of these activities themselves as they like.

The rooms appear to be clean and cosy; quietly decorated, maintaining the normal family home environment. We pass several residents getting ready to go for a walk into the township and one gentleman is pottering in the back garden; harvesting carrots for dinner. They all seem spritely and very animated. There is no one sitting staring vacantly into space.

Moira talks to Uncle, but he doesn't respond. He follows her dutifully on the tour but gives nothing away when asked about what activities he likes to pursue. I feel guilty now for not having talked this visit through with him, what must he be thinking? As Moira leads Uncle into the back garden, I stand in the doorway and watch him, trying hard to picture him living here.

'Henry looks very sad,' says Michelle, coming to stand beside me.

'He is very sad,' I respond, impressed with her intuitiveness. 'His wife, Hettie, died earlier this week.'

'Oh! I am sorry for your loss.' There is sincerity in Michelle's voice and I feel that these are not just automatic words, she is truly sorry for us both.

'Is it companionship you are after?' she asks. 'Is that why you are looking at a home for Henry?'

'No. It's…Well, I live in London, too far away to be of much use and I don't think Uncle is safe to live on his own. He gets confused; disoriented about the time of day and what he's doing.'

'Is he always like that, or only sometimes?'

'It comes and goes. He can be perfectly switched on to what's happening and where he is and then his mind just seems to wander off.'

Michelle nods. I'm sure she has seen this many times before.

'Don't let him get dehydrated,' she advises. 'A lot of people, once they get older, worry about having to go to the toilet in the night, so they don't drink anything after lunch. From my experience, these are the ones who seem to become confused and start to wander or do odd things at odd times. Just make sure Henry drinks regularly throughout the day and he should be much better. Really, it's far easier to manage one trip to the toilet each night, than hours of confusion which only leads to upsets on everyone's part.'

I thank her for her advice and vow to follow it, things can't get any worse than they already have been. Uncle and Moira return and we make our way back to the front room where we are offered tea and biscuits. Uncle refuses both.

Moira explains that there are no vacancies at present and that she usually has a waiting list, but not at the moment. Normally it could take weeks, possibly months, before she would be able to accommodate Uncle, however, a vacancy is likely to come up at the end of next week, when one of the residents will move north to be closer to their family. Without a waiting list, this room could be offered to Uncle, if we would like it. Moira should be able to confirm the details by next Tuesday.

I had not considered the possibility of no vacancies and waiting lists. Part of me feels a sense of relief that I will not have to worry about Uncle past my two-week leave of absence from work, and part of me wishes that a waiting list existed so I could keep putting off the inevitable. However, the slight delay in finding a place for Uncle will take the pressure off me, if only for a few days, in terms of making a decision. I have permission to do nothing now about a long-term solution for Uncle because there is nothing that can be done now.

I like this home, as much as it is possible to like any nursing home. Certainly, it appeals to me more than the other one did; that one was too big and seemed intent on taking away any remaining independence that the residents had. But Uncle's reaction and his current behaviour worries me. I am still unresolved as to what I want to do, but I can't afford to say no at this stage, so I agree to put Uncle's name down.

Moira asks for some personal and contact details. Uncle does not respond to any of her questions so I supply the information. Once she has Uncle's particulars, Moira turns to me.

'So, Joe, you are Henry's next-of-kin, his nephew I believe?'

'Great-nephew,' I correct.

'Yes, that's right,' pipes in Uncle suddenly, breaking his long silence. 'Joe is a great nephew. He's the greatest nephew anyone could ever have.'

Moira smiles at this, but my heart sinks. What sort of "greatest nephew anyone could ever have" would take Uncle away from his own home and house him with a bunch of strangers?

ଔଔଔଔଔ

Back at the cottage as we pass the evening in the front room, I discuss the home with Uncle. I've followed Michelle's advice and kept him well-hydrated. He seems quite lucid and so far today we've had no incidents of inappropriate comments or behaviour or any disorientation.

'What did you think of the home we visited today, Uncle?'

'Very nice for those who need to live there.'

'Can you see yourself living there?'

'I don't need to live there. I have this cottage. I have a home here with Hettie.'

This comment dismays me, obviously, Uncle is not as lucid as I thought.

'Hettie isn't here anymore, Uncle,' I gently remind him.

He gives me a sad smile.

'I know that, Joe. I know that Hettie has passed. But this cottage is all about Hettie. It's where we lived together, where we ate together, where we laughed and talked, and just were together. If I leave here, I'll lose all of that. Hettie's passing doesn't change the fact that this is my home with her.'

I struggle for a moment to think of a way to respond.

'Remember when Father died and you told me that it didn't matter where I went or what I did in life as long as I carried a memory of him in my heart, he would always be with me?' Uncle nods slowly. 'Well, it's the same for you and Hettie.'

Uncle sighs.

'True,' he acknowledges. 'But it's a natural progression for a child to leave their parents and go on with their own life. Admittedly, in dying so early, Gerald did not give you the opportunity to move away first. However, my advice in that case is still relevant. It's different for me, though, because Hettie was my partner. We were supposed to live out our life here together. I don't ever want to lose her'

Uncle's sadness brings tears to my eyes and I am unable to think of any words in response. He too falls silent for a moment as two tears roll gently down his cheeks.

'I forget things sometimes, Joe. I'm scared if I leave here I'll forget my memories of Hettie. I couldn't bear to do that. That's why I've got to stay here.'

'It's okay, Uncle. I won't let that happen. We'll find a way to keep you here, safe and sound in this cottage.'

Realistically, I have no idea how I can do this. I have a wife and a job in London. I cannot forsake either of those and even if Uncle wanted to come with me, I know that he will never settle back into life in the city. The thought of being within the township of Charmouth is enough to unsettle him. Am I making promises that I cannot keep?

Chapter 18

'Uncle. Uncle, are you awake?'

Dawn is only just breaking as I rouse Uncle from his sleep, but already I can tell it is going to be a beautiful day. Uncle is facing towards me, sleeping peacefully with one arm thrown over, almost protectively, to Hettie's side of the bed. He stirs at the sound of my voice. I wait for his eyes to focus before I continue. As Michelle predicted, we've had a better night, only one, quick, trip to the toilet, which Uncle managed by himself with me listening anxiously from my bedroom, and no other disturbances.

'Would you like to go out exploring?' I ask him when I am sure he is fully awake. He gives a little smile and rises slowly to his feet. I leave him to shower and dress while I go downstairs to make breakfast. By the time we are ready to head out, the sun if fully above the horizon. The sky is a pale blue colour and cloud-free.

'What did you have in mind?' Uncle asks me as he joins me on the back porch. He is dressed in his tatty old coat and has donned his sun hat.

I have given this idea a lot of thought during the many hours I lay awake after Uncle's trip to the toilet. Maybe it is unrealistic of me to think I can keep Uncle here in this cottage, especially with me looking after him. But I know I have another ten days of leave left, and why not try to make it the best ten days we ever had.

'I thought we might go to the beach and play Robinson Crusoe,' I respond and Uncle grins.

Jess trots along beside us as we make our way through the back gate and across the field of long grass. At the top of the cliffs, we stop and look out across the sea. There is a light breeze ruffling the surface and only small waves lap at the shore. We turn right and walk down the path towards the River Char. At the end of the path, we remove our shoes and toss them into the grass.

The river flow across the beach and into the sea is not deep and we both easily wade across. The water is chilly though and our feet are blue by the time we reach the other side. Slowly, we make our way along the beach collecting shells and seaweed as we go. At the end of our walk, we've found four different types of seaweed and twelve different types of shells.

When we reach the river for our return crossing, Uncle wanders down to the sea's edge and lets the waves wash over his feet.

'You were fascinated by the waves that first day I brought you here.'

'I'd never seen the sea before. This was all new to me, a true adventure.'

'You truly were Robinson Crusoe back then.' Uncle says as he turns to me and together with Jess, we make our way home.

The day has been good for me; a peaceful and pleasant time with Uncle. I feel no sense of the stress that has plagued me since the day of Hettie's phone call. I have no idea how I'm going to keep my promise to Uncle, but I've decided not to worry about that now. I just want a few days to reconnect with Uncle and the days of my childhood, we can worry about everything else after that.

The following morning, after another good night, we set out for Golden Cap. The clouds have returned and although it is not cold, the threat of rain hangs in the air. The first drops start to fall before we have begun our climb to the top, so we turn and head for home.

'Good thing too,' says Uncle. 'I'm not sure I have the energy to race you to the top at my age.'

'I thought you were doing well to do that twenty years ago,' I respond with a laugh.

On the third day, we go prospecting on East Beach. The sun comes and goes behind a series of fluffy white clouds, but the day stays fine. We search amongst the shale, finding only partial fossils of ammonites.

'I used to dream about discovering a dinosaur skeleton,' I confess to Uncle.

'I did too. There's still a chance that you might. Because of the coastal erosion, new and unexplored areas are now becoming accessible.'

'I won't give up on my dream then.'

'No,' responds Uncle emphatically. 'You should never do that.'

We move on to fossick for an hour through the rock pools. Jess makes herself comfortable on the rocks that have been warmed by the sun and sleeps. Uncle reminds me of how I used to try and rescue the little fish that had been stranded by the receding tide. We both laugh at that memory and embark on a flood of others.

'Remember when we fell in the river fully clothed?'

'What about the time we found Mrs Brown, Peggy, Gertie, and Willow on the side of the road? We must have made a funny sight as we were trying to catch them.'

'How about when we went star gazing and Hettie was cross with you because we fell asleep and woke covered in dew and both ended up with a cold?'

'I remember. I think Hettie was cross with me a lot in those days. What was it she used to call me?'

'Incorrigible,' I reply.

'That's right. And it's true. I was incorrigible, but boy did we have some fun.'

'We did, Uncle. We did.'

As the warmth of the sun starts to wane, we make our way slowly home. Jess, who was reluctant to wake, plods along wearily behind us, and I wonder if I should leave her at home in the future. Despite the pills Clara has left for her, she is an old dog and the stiffness in her joints from the arthritis limits her movements. Uncle also seems to have slowed his pace and it is dark by the time we reach home. I worry that I have been asking too much of them both with these adventures and even though I still want to reach the top of Golden Cap; resolve that tomorrow should be a rest day.

That night, Uncle gets up to the toilet twice. I hear him both times, my mind now programmed to wake the instant I hear him stir. I do not go to assist him, just listen to make sure everything is alright. After the second visit, I hear him pause outside my bedroom door. I've taken to leaving it open to better my chances of hearing him.

'Joe.'

'Yes, Uncle.'

'Is it morning time yet?'

'Not yet. It's only a little after four, plenty of sleep time left yet.'

'Okay.' With that, he patters back to bed.

When I arise the next morning, Jess is nowhere to be seen. Usually, she sleeps curled up on the front porch; she has never liked the kennel that Uncle and Hettie provided. When she hears the first movement in the house, she usually makes her way to the back porch in anticipation of being given her breakfast and taken on the morning walk.

This morning, she is not at the back door. Thinking she may not have heard me, I check the front porch but she is not there either. Uncle joins me and together we search the garden. Uncle is the one to find her, under one of the old apple trees. It is a favourite spot of hers, he explains, one where she could easily snack on the low-growing apples. Jess is conscious but incapable of movement. Her brown eyes look at me pleadingly.

I so desperately wish that Clara was here with me now, but she is not and there is little assistance she can offer me from London. I leave Uncle with Jess and head to the cottage to call the local vet. Then I return outside to sit with Uncle who is lying on the grass beside Jess, just gently patting her. The vet, a very pleasant young man with better bedside manners than I have seen in many doctors, arrives within the half hour.

'Jess has had a stroke,' he explains to Uncle, correctly identifying him as the dog's master. 'She isn't in any pain, but she has lost the ability to move. I'm sorry, sir, but I won't be able to make her better, I can only help her passing.'

'I understand,' says Uncle. 'She's been a loyal and beautiful companion, she deserves the best of care. You do what you have to.'

We both stay with Jess as the vet administers the injection. Jess is placid, looking up trustingly at Uncle, never looking away from his face. After some minutes, she gives a deep sigh and the light fades from her eyes.

Uncle does not cry, but I struggle to maintain my composure as I walk the vet back to his car and thank him for coming so quickly.

Uncle and I agree to bury Jess next to where Floss lies. Uncle stays with her, gently stroking her fur, while I dig the hole. We wrap her in her blanket and lower her into her final resting place. Uncle thanks her for being such a beautiful and faithful companion and then goes to gather some flowers to adorn her grave while I replace the dirt.

'This afternoon, I'll make a headstone, like the one we have for Floss.'

'That would be nice. Thanks, Joe.'

Uncle plods sadly into the cottage and I follow at a distance. Inside, I head for the phone to call Clara to tell her what has happened.

'I think I pushed her too much,' I tell Clara. 'She seemed so much fitter these last few days without the burden of the arthritis.'

Clara reassures me that I haven't caused her any harm. Jess was just old and her time had come, but these words do little to ease my sense of guilt.

Uncle, who has been sitting on the couch staring at nothing, gets up and comes over to where I am sitting by the phone and puts his arm around my shoulder.

'It's not your fault, Joe,' he tells me. 'Jess just missed Hettie and wanted to go to her.'

The thought of Jess and Hettie together makes me feel slightly better, it is good to think that Hettie is no longer alone.

We go through the motions of the rest of the day's routine. Although both of us only pick at food, I still make sure that Uncle continues to drink well throughout the day. The night is more challenging, but not because of any untoward incidents on Uncle's part. He is simply reluctant to go to bed, unable to settle. I do not feel that I can leave him up alone, and so I too spend hours either sitting or roaming around, but either way, achieving nothing. It is after three in the morning before we finally retire for the night, but I don't think either of us sleeps.

ৡৡৡৡৡৡ

It is Uncle who suggests the following morning that we should complete our journey to Golden Cap. Once again, it surprises me, this moment of lucidity, of remembering what we started but hadn't finished. Maybe it's the extra fluids I've been giving him, or maybe it's just a brief remission from the deterioration that is dementia, but I feel overall Uncle's mind has been more focused than not in the last couple of days. Possibly though, it's simply down to the fact that we've spent these days reliving the past, a place he knows more deeply than the present.

'I won't race you to the top, but I'm sure if we take it at a steady pace I can make it all the way there.'

The day is clear, warm and bright with no threat of rain. I don't believe I can spend any longer confined within the four walls of the cottage after yesterday, so I am only too happy to agree. It feels odd to walk this familiar route without a dog trotting along beside us, but I try not to think of that.

Uncle's pace is steady and unhurried. Though I could move faster, I temper my pace to suit his. Slowly, we make the ascent and I feel it is with a sense of relief on Uncle's part that we finally reach our usual sitting place. Warmed by the walk and the beating of the sun, I remove my jacket and Uncle sheds his coat. We sit side by side, staring out at the view.

'Joe.'

'Yes, Uncle.'

'Do you think you've had a good life?' Uncle suddenly asks me.

I ponder my response for a minute. Not everything about my childhood was a bed of roses, but I don't feel any the worse for the experience.

'Yes, I think so,' I finally respond.

'I've had a good life you know, especially since I've lived in Charmouth. Coming here was the best thing for me, it helped me put things in perspective.'

'How so?'

'I got confused when I was young and that set me off on the wrong path in life. I wanted to help everyone, I wanted to make everyone happy, to take away all the sadness that had afflicted us during the great war. I thought that happiness meant having no worries and that having no worries was dependent on financial stability. I don't mean that we all have to have pots of money to be happy, but that we could be happy if we didn't have to live forever stressing about how to pay the bills.

'I'd seen some bad things, Joe, some sad situations both before and after the war. Widows were kicked out of their homes because the house was tied to the job and if they had no husband to do the job, they had no right to be in the house anymore. Kids starving and going barefoot in winter. Men, maimed in the service of their country, and then relegated to the scrap heap because of their injuries. It was not nice.

'And overseas, gosh, what I saw in places like India and Africa, it breaks my heart to think of it now. Such horrible poverty! Even in wealthier countries like the United States, they have people who can't afford basic medical care. To my mind, that's not right.

'Anyway, I looked at all the sad situations I'd seen and I kept thinking all of their problems would be solved if these people just had sufficient money to get by. They could be worry-free and, consequently, happy then.'

'You don't believe that anymore?'

'Money helps, I don't deny that, but it's not the universal panacea I thought it should be. You taught me that, Joe.'

'I did?'

'Absolutely. That first day you arrived, when I got you off the bus, you were so sad then. But you didn't need money to make you happy.'

'No,' I agree, reflecting on that time. 'I just needed love and companionship.'

'Well, actually, what you needed right then was to know that it was okay to pee in the bushes.'

I laugh. The memory of that moment is sweet. I can feel again my consternation that I might wet my pants but if I went to the toilet in public Mother wouldn't like it. Uncle smiles at my amusement, the first smile I've seen from him for days.

'You needed to pee and when you'd done that you were happy. Then you needed to know that you hadn't been sent to us as a punishment for something you'd done wrong. Once you knew that you were happy. Then yes, you needed love and companionship, and breakfast, and adventures, and to know the joy of scones with piles of jam and cream. They were such little things and I could give you all of that. I could make you worry-free and happy.

'Your life in London with Helen, your mother, wasn't…well, wasn't always happy, but you could come here for the summers and know that all you ever needed to make you happy was right here in Charmouth. You didn't need to go looking anywhere else for it. I feared that going overseas, seeing all the sad things might upset you, like it upset me. I feared you might lose the sense of happiness that can be gained from the little things. You didn't need to make the search for happiness any more than it should be, you already had it. I so badly wanted you to understand that.'

'I did know that, Uncle. You and Hettie, my summers here, they were my lifeline. It wasn't happiness that I was looking for when I left here when I travelled overseas. It was life. It was experiences and adventures, something different to what I already knew.

'You did achieve what you set out to do, Uncle. You might not have made the whole world happy, but Floss, Jess, Hettie, and I are all certainly the better for your efforts. I, for one, would have been a totally different person, a very sad and lonely person, if I hadn't had you as my lifeline during my childhood.'

Uncle reaches out to hold my hand.

'I'm glad of that, Joe. It means a lot to me to hear you say it. I believe Hettie would be pleased too.'

We sit for a while in silence, just looking at the vastness of the sea. Finally, Uncle stirs and gets unsteadily to his feet, turning himself in the direction of the cottage.

'I think I'm ready to go now, Lad. I need to go and talk to Hettie, to tell her what you said.'

Epilogue

Uncle passes away that night. He slips away peacefully sometime during the dark hours. I don't know if I was awake or asleep at the time, but I was unaware of him going.

I find him in the morning, lying on his side of the bed, with his arm resting where Hettie should have been. I know immediately that he has gone; I can tell by the relaxed, peaceful expression he has on his face. I haven't seen him look like that in such a long time. I sit on the stool at Hettie's dressing table and watch over him for a long time before finally going downstairs to phone Dr Gregg.

I worry that, like with Jess, I have hastened Uncle's death by all our activities of the past few days. But I think I understand his passing. Uncle, like Jess, just wanted to be with Hettie.

I also worry if I'd cared for him as well as I could have, the role of carer was not really one that I felt I'd had a natural aptitude for. But when I think of our last conversation on Golden Cap, I feel that in these last days, I was able to give back to Uncle exactly what he had given to me. Just like, as a five years old boy, all I needed to know was that it was okay to pee in the bushes, at the end all Uncle needed to know was that he had achieved in his life some of what he had set out to do.

Initially, I feel totally bereft and abandoned, but Clara's arrival reminds me that my life and destiny is linked with her, not with Uncle. Hettie and Uncle will always be the most influential people I have ever encountered in my life, but our paths were only ever meant to converge for a short time; not for a lifetime.

Uncle's funeral is a quiet affair, once again Dr Gregg is the only other mourner to join Clara and I. In my eulogy, I focus mostly on recounting some of Uncle's and my adventures together. I both laughed and cry as I describe them. To give him the full tribute that he deserves, though, I do make reference to his years of study and work in the field of social welfare.

The day after the funeral, I am contacted by a solicitor. To continue the legacy they started when I was only five years old, Uncle and Hettie have left me their cottage in Stonebarrow Lane. I know that it will be difficult to visit here initially, but I hope that in time I too will have a young child with whom I can share the joys of playing at being Robinson Crusoe.